FOREVER IN MY HEART

DIONNE GRACE

Copyright

Forever in my Heart
Copyright © 2020 Dionne Grace
All rights reserved.

All scripture quotations are taken from The Holy Bible, New International Version.
Published by: Dionne Grace
Visit the author's website at:
www.dionnegrace.com

Dedication

To my Lord God who never fails.

Prologue

Sherry Palmer listened to the gentle rustle of the trees and green foliage in the distance. She closed her eyes as a rush of wind brushed against her face, heightening her excitement at what was about to take place. Music flowed through her spirit, bursting forth as a symphony of sound in worship and thanksgiving to the Lord.

She sang to the melody: *"How wonderful you are! I give you all my praise. I am nothing without you, my awesome Lord of glory. I just want to be with you. I can't breathe without you…"*

As she continued to sing, she saw the words float from her lips and ascend into the sky, to an open heaven above.

As though in answer, angels descended one by one, gathering by her balcony window and seeming to wait for her prayers.

Her spirit stirred. She said a prayer that had whispered in her heart for so long.

Lord, I pray that one day you will be merciful and show me how he is.

She felt her heart quicken, and within her spirit there was an awareness—*a knowing* of something that would someday be revealed.

Sherry continued to pray in thanksgiving. God's presence was powerful and overwhelming. Tears came to her eyes, and then, to her surprise, one of the angels appeared beside her. He seemed to glow, a radiant light surrounding him. He raised a hand, and suddenly there was a bright flash and a vision appeared before her.

The hospital room was white: the walls, the bed, the sheets. The haze cleared from the brightness of the sun streaming through the window to reveal a woman in bed holding a baby boy.

"Thank you," Adrian said simply. There were tears in his eyes.

The woman looked down at the baby and smiled.

Too soon, the vision ended and the angels were gone. Stunned for a moment, Sherry took a seat.

What are you showing me, Lord? Who is the woman? She couldn't quite work it out. Although she'd seen the woman smile, when she tried to look closer to take in her face, it was obscured from her view.

"Pray for Adrian, Sherry," Holy Spirit said.

Adrian.

She thought of him often. Today was no different.

Sherry blinked and looked out of the hotel balcony. She took in the beautiful burnt sky with rich hues of red blended with oranges, and a splash of yellow to set off the artistic display. The spectacular Blue Mountains and lush green landscapes in the distance transported her into fond memories of love.

Adrian Chase had been her first love. He'd been the *only* man she'd ever loved. He wasn't suave or sophisticated, but he was handsome, in a quiet kind of way, and he'd *adored* her. And she'd adored him.

Sherry met him when she attended university, and her life had never been the same. He'd changed something within her and made her feel like a *real* woman—special and unique.

He was *everything*. More than she could ever have hoped for. He'd swept her off her feet, and she'd fallen deeply in love. She didn't know what had hit her and was totally unprepared for the way he stole her heart. Every time he looked at her with his gorgeous, dark, intense brown eyes, she melted. And when he drew her into his arms one night under the stars and asked her to spend the rest of her life with him, her heart had leapt and her eyes welled with tears.

Then, on bended knee, he'd asked her to marry him, and she'd said yes, because living a life without him would be a life not worth living.

On a sigh, Sherry returned her gaze to the amazing view of Jamaica and its natural wonders before her. She was grateful and thanked God for the pleasure. She visited every year because she knew Adrian loved it here.

Her heart ached, and her eyes misted with tears. The pain had never left.

She missed him.

Still, she was alive; she had breath—except she wasn't living. She was only but a shell without him…

<u>1</u>

Sherry wondered, what if she'd married him? What would her life have been like? They would have had three children by now. That was the number they'd decided on—two girls and one boy. He'd said he wanted the girls to be miniatures of her, and the boy to be a miniature of him. Adrian had even said that there could be no one else—only *she* would be the mother to his children—and she'd *believed* him. They had been perfect together, and she knew they would have been happy, married and settled with a family. They'd talked about it enough.

Still, there was no point in speculating. He was lost to her. She'd heard he'd gotten married and started a family. It hurt when she found out, a vicelike pain that had seized her heart and had never let go. And God had even sent the vision as confirmation, that he had the baby boy he'd always wanted.

Regrettably, she'd reached a plateau in her life. At thirty-eight, she still felt like she was twenty-five, with a whole lot of love and nurturing to give.

Where had the time gone?

What was she supposed to do about the desperation she often felt at the knowledge that she would soon be forty? She'd never been a wife or mother; she'd always professed to her friends and family that it wasn't her purpose in life, even though she knew deep down that it was a ruse to make herself feel better about the emptiness she felt inside. She used it as a fallback phrase to somehow deflect the looks of pity that came her way.

Her body was no longer as firm as it used to be. She couldn't compete with younger women, but she was attractive, and still got satisfaction from a few interested looks from men when she made an effort to go out. Although she often wondered at those looks, if they were only contemplative speculation of what she may have looked like when she was younger.

There had been a few dates over the years, but they never really amounted to anything.

Why?

Because she was still in love with Adrian.

He'd never left her heart, and thereafter, every man she got close to, she couldn't help but make comparisons to him. They always fell short.

At her age, she'd missed the boat where children were concerned. After things ended with Adrian, she'd always thought she would meet someone else and have a large family, filled with a horde of kids. She never second-guessed it; it had always been *expected*. Now, it was too late. Although it wasn't entirely misplaced to consider a woman in her late thirties starting a family, but who would she even contemplate marrying right now?

She chuckled as she thought of Lyle, a business associate whom she dated occasionally when neither had anything better to do. He was pleasant, *sometimes*. And when he wasn't, she tuned him out.

Lyle was *miserable*. That was the only word she could think of that she could even begin to regard as suitable for him. If she let him, a whole evening would be spent discussing the reason he thought the world would come to an end. Everything was *so* dramatic. He was definitely a glass-half-empty type of man—a real *joy* to be with at times.

Sherry recalled when he first began visiting her. The dark spirit around him would become unsettled and try to cause an argument between them. One night he came to pick her up and stood by the door, becoming agitated, trying to rush her, annoyed that she was late. She knew why he was agitated; it was because of the angel that stood guard at her door.

Saying a silent prayer within, she watched as the angel did his work. He was tall—well over seven feet. He looked like a powerful armoured soldier, his thick, strong arms folded as he peered down at Lyle. Lyle couldn't see him, but as soon as the angel moved to touch Lyle's shoulder, she saw the dark spirit flee. It didn't even wait for the angel's hand to touch Lyle; it was gone in a flash.

Lyle's demeanour changed straight away; his eyes brightened and a glow seemed to form around him. It was the most beautiful sight. It brought tears to her eyes.

That night, she spoke to Lyle about God, but he wasn't ready. Even so, she knew that, in time, he would be.

Lyle was okay to look at and would occasionally stand proudly by her side when she attended company functions. Nevertheless, they didn't have a lot in common. She was convinced he was seeing someone else—not that she minded. Their relationship had never progressed further than an awkward kiss on the cheek, and they hadn't made any commitments to each other. He definitely wasn't marrying material, so she was destined, it would seem, for a life on her own. That saddened her, except her purpose, she knew, was as a conduit for God to do a work in Lyle. He was softening, but it was slow.

Pushing those thoughts aside, she figured she'd better get a move on, otherwise she would be late for work. She headed to the bathroom for a quick shower. When she was done, she stood in front of the wardrobe and wondered what she should wear. She was meeting with the board today, so a suit would suffice. Pulling one out, she stepped into the trousers and then tried to zip them up.

Sherry groaned. She'd put on weight—comfort eating, for sure. Most nights now, she'd been dreaming about Adrian, and the memories just wouldn't cease. So snacking had become a habit that she needed to stop.

Looking at herself in the mirror, she made a rapid assessment: her stomach was still flat, but her hips and backside were a little curvier. She needed to go on a diet. This would not do. She rummaged in her wardrobe again for a looser pair of trousers and then dressed quickly for work.

As she gave herself one more look in the mirror, she could feel Him. So she took a moment and closed her eyes and prayed. His presence filled the room, and all she could do was cry. He overwhelmed her, and when He said, *"I love you, Sherry,"* more tears came to her eyes.

She replied, *"I love you too, my Lord,"* and basked in the awesome, wondrous power of His presence. Only then was she ready for her day.

Grabbing her handbag and her Christian Louboutin heels, she made her way downstairs to the living room, sat on the sofa, and slipped them on while she thought about her plan for the day. Marketing was the main agenda. Their website and brand needed a total overhaul. She wondered what the consensus would be. Her team *loathed* any notion of change.

On a sigh, she headed for the kitchen in desperate need of a cup of tea. She was definitely going to need it. The shrill of her phone diverted her attention, and she fished it out of her handbag.

Candace.

Sherry answered.

"Are you packed yet?" Candace asked.

"No, not yet."

"We're leaving tomorrow. Get organised."

"I know, I know." Sherry tried to summon some kind of enthusiasm for their trip, but no matter how much she'd tried, she just couldn't. Still, it was a week of beautiful sun, sea, and sand. Maybe when she got on the plane her fervour would increase.

Their friend Marcie was getting married to her partner, Jake, of sixteen years. Theirs was an ardent love, and they had a brood of kids to show for it. Most of Sherry's friends were married. She'd become relegated to Aunty Sherry, who brought gifts for their children whenever she visited. Even Candace had been married, but was now divorced, and two teenage boys later, was on the lookout for husband number two. Sherry wished her all the luck in the world.

She crossed the living area and opened the curtains, allowing light to pour into the room. Warm colours graced the walls, in contrast to the white sofas and carpet. This room was the favourite in her home. It calmed her.

"Oh, come on, Sherry. We're going to sunny Jamaica, your favourite place. Why don't you sound happier about this?"

It was true. Sherry loved Jamaica, but she liked to go on her own, with no distractions, taking in the beautiful scenery and hiking the mountains at her leisure. Not stuck in a hotel at a wedding reception. "Because we're attending a wedding, and you know how I feel about weddings. I don't even think I've got anything to wear."

"Yeah, right. This coming from the designer queen of the century. Let me loose in *your* wardrobe and I'll find something for you, me, and half of London."

Sherry chuckled, walked through to the kitchen, and switched on the kettle. "I'm hardly the designer queen, you have a fair few in your wardrobe from what I remember and besides, that's only if I can find anything to fit me. I've put on weight."

Her friend laughed. "Really? How much? A pound? The day you put on weight is the day that I'm a size ten, and you know *that* will never happen."

Candace was beautiful and big. She loved her size and never apologised for it. And men loved her, so why would she want to? She had a big personality that drew men in. Everyone loved her.

Sherry smiled. "I have put on weight, believe it or not, but I'll take it off once I step up my exercise."

"I'm rolling my eyes down the phone. Anyway, you've probably already had your workout, written twenty reports, and are only now thinking about a cup of tea."

Candace knew her so well. Yes, Sherry's day began with prayer, then down at the gym, and when she returned, she did a couple of hours on her laptop. She was a confirmed workaholic. It was her business—well, hers and her father's—so she couldn't afford a day off. "What do you want me to say? It's true. You know my routine."

"Well, you had better leave that laptop at home. It's supposed to be a week away to have fun and relax. Take a break for once in your life."

Yeah, like that's ever going to happen. "I hear you, Candace. What time am I meeting you at the airport?"

<u>2</u>

Adrian handed her a bouquet and a box of chocolates as he met her at her door. Sherry grinned and kissed him on his cheek. She brought the beautiful collection of vibrant flowers to her nose. "Thank you," she said wistfully, then felt the sting in her eyes as she became choked with emotion. He was sweet to her, always so considerate.

He looked good today, too, in faded jeans and a shirt that hugged his muscular frame. She liked the way the white of his shirt enhanced his smooth, creamy latte skin tone. His light jacket gave him a stylish look. Although it was summer, the evenings tended to cool considerably, which was the reason she'd eventually decided on jeans too. She couldn't make up her mind on what to wear, knowing Adrian would notice.

Oh, she was aware that men generally "noticed," but Adrian was more observant than most.

The fact that he took an interest in what she wore had thrown her at first. Typically, the guys she dated would say the usual, "You look pretty" or "You're looking nice, Sherry," and leave it at that, but not Adrian. While he would say those things too, he went a little further, saying her outfit looked elegant or sophisticated, or comment on how the colour she was wearing accentuated the rich mocha of her skin tone. He certainly had a way with words and made her feel special.

The blouse she'd chosen today was maroon with flecks of gold. He'd told her once that the colour suited her, as it "reflected in her beautiful brown eyes." She remembered how his eyes had become all intense as he took her in, making her skin tingle all over, and she couldn't help the smile that tugged at her lips.

Even as she looked at him now, he made her feel giddy. She could see the light in his eyes as he stared at her.

"You look incredible, Sherry." He took her hand and brought it to his chest. "You're making my heart race. Can you feel it?"

She smiled, and a warmth radiated inside, setting off butterflies in her tummy. "Yes," she said, and because she was embarrassed by the intense look in his eyes, she asked, "Where are you taking me?"

He gave her a mischievous look. "It's a surprise."

As they stood on her doorstep talking, it wasn't long before she could feel eyes on them through the windows to her home. No doubt her mother and sister were watching from the bedrooms above.

In his hand he held another bouquet. She wondered why, until he said, "Before we go, I need to speak to your mother first. Can I come in for a moment?"

She frowned. "But why?"

He smiled. "Don't be worried. I need to ask her permission to date you."

"What?" She looked at him in disbelief as he stepped over the threshold. "You don't need to do that," she said, lowering her voice to a whisper. They'd already been dating for a couple of months, so there was no need for this, and besides, it was embarrassing.

"Yes, I do," he said.

And then, to make matters worse, Angela, her younger sister, descended the staircase. As suspected, she'd been watching them.

Mortified at what Adrian had just proposed, Sherry drew him aside. "You don't need to do this," she whispered.

But before he could respond, her mother also descended with a flair only she could pull off—considering fifteen minutes before she was in a dressing gown and rollers—wearing a fuchsia maxi dress and fluffy pink slippers. And to complete the look, her hair was a mass of curls around her face and shoulders. "Hello, young man," she said.

Adrian smiled. "Hello, Mrs Palmer." He handed her the flowers. "A gift for you."

She grinned, taking them from him. Sherry could see the admiration in her mother's eyes. Adrian got that a lot. Most women were taken by him and his quiet charm.

"It's nice to meet you, finally," her mother said, putting an emphasis on the last word.

Sherry's mother had been badgering her to bring Adrian home for dinner. Sherry hadn't been ready for that—she still wasn't.

Adrian held out a hand towards her mother, intending to take hers.

"Why so formal?" her mother asked with a smile, and drew him into a hug. "Since the day you met, my daughter has *been walking around the house smiling and daydreaming, like she hasn't got a care in the world. I've been wanting to meet you for a while."*

"Mum." Sherry groaned in embarrassment.

Adrian smiled, looking at Sherry. "That's good to know."

"Don't you use that against me," Sherry warned him.

"Hello," Angela said shyly. She'd been standing beside her mother but stepped forward to make her presence known. Angela was seventeen and not ready for the adult world that awaited her and was so very shy of boys. She was in her normal attire of jeans and a t-shirt with some nondescript logo, intentionally loose to hide her developing body.

Angela was pretty, and although they had similarities between them, she took after their mother, whereas Sherry took after their father. Angela's complexion was lighter, but they both had chocolate-brown eyes.

Adrian grinned. "Hey. Sherry's told me all about you."

Angela smiled.

"She told me your favourite author is Danielle Steel, and I just happened to come across a copy of one of her books." He handed it to her.

Angela grinned, taking it from him. "Thank you! I haven't read this one yet! Mum, look." Angela showed her mother the book, then stepped into Adrian and hugged him, her head barely reaching his chest.

Sherry smiled, and the choked-up feeling she felt inside threatened to overwhelm her. She looked at Adrian, her heart filled with joy and gratitude. He'd brought smiles to the two most important people in her life.

She loved him.

Sherry felt the atmosphere change. The heaviness that sometimes hovered in the air seemed to release, and a vibrant light formed around them.

They couldn't see that, of course. Only she could, and in that moment, she knew he was the one she wanted to spend the rest of her life with.

* * *

Does he ever think of me, Lord?

Sherry waited for an answer, but none came.

Did he whisper her name in the middle of the night? Did he ever dream of her as she dreamt of him?

Sherry remembered one night when they'd gone to the cinema for retro night to see her favourite film, *Forrest Gump*. And because he was so sweet, kind, and considerate, he bought her the DVD for her birthday and then teased her when she wanted to watch it over and over again. She wondered if he thought of her whenever he saw that film.

"Do you think of me, Adrian?" she whispered in the darkness. "I miss you." She turned on her side and closed her eyes and tried to sleep, but it did not dispel the memories of him or the ache in her heart.

She felt discontented, like there had to be more to life than this.

Is this it, Lord?

She wasn't unhappy, just lonely sometimes—not because she was alone, but because she missed Adrian. She'd missed him for *fifteen years* and wondered when the ache inside would ever leave.

Turning, she glanced at the clock on the nightstand, and wasn't surprised to see that it was one a.m. She'd been unsettled all day at work. Nevertheless, she needed to sleep, and had to be up at four if she was going to make it to the airport on time. She could finish that report…

Her day had been hectic, and maybe that was why she couldn't sleep. Even though she was confident her staff were proficient and able to run things smoothly while she was away, she still felt an uneasiness in her soul. Something always went wrong, leaving her no choice but to resolve it while on holiday.

She would finish the report on the plane. The deadline wasn't for another week, so she had time. Her thoughts drifted, and she was reminded of the day they met.

* * *

It was a grey day in September, and it was drizzling. Her hair was beginning to frizz. It was because of this that she kept her hair short. She just didn't have the patience for styling long hair. Besides, her newly cut bob looked good and showed off her face. Maybe she would go shorter next time. She would see.

She was pretty; she acknowledged that. She didn't have an outstanding beauty, but it would do. She was never one for preening, like her friends did. "Wash and go" was her motto. She sometimes wore makeup if she could be bothered, but her main focus was her studies. She was a straight-A student and boys were at the bottom of her list of things to do, unlike her friends, who seemed to think going out partying to meet boys was the be-all and end-all of life.

Sherry couldn't afford to live on site, so rented a room nearby. It was within walking distance and good exercise in the mornings. She also had time to gather her thoughts for the day and listen to the birds sing. It was a delightful way to start her day.

Rushing to campus, she checked her watch. She'd been up studying for her financial management exam until the early hours, and now she was late. Although tired and a little frazzled at the edges, she was confident she would achieve a grade that would put her at the top of her class.

Sherry stepped out in the road, and her mobile buzzed. She looked down at the face and the text from Marcie.

Where are you?

I'm coming.

But where are you?

She shifted her handbag on her shoulder and went to reply, but then felt a strong arm grab her by the waist and pull her backwards with such a force that she lost her footing. She found herself being held up by a solid hunk of a man of pure muscle and bulk. She realised belatedly, as a bus sped by just inches from her, that she'd narrowly escaped being struck.

"Are you okay?" he asked.

Disorientated, she turned, looking up, and recognised the man from her dreams. God had told her about him. He had said they would become friends and that she must tell him about Jesus. This wasn't out of the ordinary for her. The Holy Spirit often wanted her to talk to strangers, friends, anyone that was open. Sometimes it would be a specific word, and other times on general terms. But unlike all the other times

God had used her, she didn't feel this undeniable chemistry. While his hold on her relaxed, he seemed reluctant to release her, and for some reason she wanted to stay right there in his arms.

He was handsome, more rugged than beautiful, light-skinned, with dark, wavy hair, a straight European nose, a square jaw, and beautiful, thick lips. His intense brown eyes pulled at her. He looked mixed race, and she wondered for a moment at his heritage.

The moment seemed to last forever as their gazes locked and time stood still. He was tall, but so was she, so he didn't tower over her, and she liked that. She could look him in his eyes, dead on.

She touched a hand to his chest, and she remembered. He was one of God's chosen, full of possibilities. He just needed to be guided in the right way. His heart was open and ready. She felt the electrical charge that seemed to bounce off him to her.

Sherry took in a breath. "Thank you. I didn't see the bus. You saved my life."

A small smile came to his lips. "Yes, it would appear. You know what that means, don't you?" His eyes flickered with amusement.

Heat raced through her veins, making her weak at the knees. "Yes, we're tied together for life."

His smile broadened. He had a beautiful smile that lit up his whole face. "Exactly," he said.

And ever since that day, they'd been tied. He'd never left her heart.

<u>3</u>

Sherry glanced around the busy airport, waiting in the long queue in departures, wanting to board already. They had been standing in line for an *age*.

She tried not to tune into the argument the couple were having ahead of them, but it was difficult because they were becoming loud, and the dark spirit that appeared beside them just made the situation worse. A storm was brewing.

"You said you had all the passports!" The man raised his voice as he watched his wife frantically search through her bags. She looked stressed out. Her long blonde hair was a mess, falling into her face every so often, and she would impatiently brush it aside as if swatting a fly. Their three children were running about, and the youngest one was now screaming.

"Gosh, I hope there wasn't ever an occasion that me and Malcolm did that in public," Candace remarked. "If fact, no, we didn't. We had enough of those indoors." She smiled.

Sherry looked at her. Candace wore jeans that emphasized her full shapely figure, and a floral cami-vest. "You make it sound as if they were fond memories."

Candace grinned cheekily. "Oh, they were, because of the way we made up afterwards."

Sherry chuckled and stepped forward with the slowly moving crowd, her gaze returning to the couple.

"You expect me to do *everything*! I had to sort out the kids. What were *you* doing? Looking at your phone, as always!" the woman barked at him.

Her husband's eyes narrowed at that, and the dark spirit whispered something to him. He was about to do something unpleasant.

Sherry prayed for the family. God only allowed her to "see" when there was a purpose, and right now it was to pray for peace.

As soon as she did, the child stopped screaming. The wife suddenly found the missing passports with a smile of relief, and her husband gave her a hug. *Storm over.* Sherry smiled within. *Thank you, Holy Spirit.*

"Thank you, Sherry," Holy Spirit said.

They finally proceeded through departures and boarded the plane. Sherry was reminded of another time when she was privy to another argument, only she wasn't able to save that one.

* * *

The first time she knew some of God's plans for Adrian's life was when he first held her hand. They were meeting at Dominica's restaurant for a study debate with a few of their friends, which were always lively.

He met her after their final lecture for the day, and they walked along Colin's Lane, sharing anecdotes from their classes.

When they came to a crossing, he took her hand with ease, as if they were old friends, and she felt the connection.

She felt him.

The pull was so strong. His hand was firm, enveloping hers, and then she felt a sizzle rush along her arm like electricity, and before she knew what was happening, her heart was racing out of control and heat swept along her skin. She knew he felt it too, because he stopped for a moment and stared at her. Then, suddenly, she was somewhere else, transported to his home.

Two dark spirits had entered. His father had arrived home drunk, and a cloud of oppression took hold. His blonde hair was unkempt and flopped in his face as he staggered in, a bottle of Jack Daniel's in his hand. His suit looked as if it had seen better days.

She could see his mother, and an argument ensued. She was angry, her face contorted in rage. She was well dressed in a navy suit and pearls, which seemed out of place in contrast to the way she was behaving—she was neither pure nor demure. Sherry couldn't tell what the argument was about, but she could feel the wrath, the bitterness and resentment that had been cultivated over a sustained period of time.

As they argued, with raised voices and vindictive, hurtful words, the oppression swelled in the room and even more dark spirits entered. By this time, what had been two had multiplied into six.

An ominous cloud descended and swirled like a tornado, the atmosphere intent and evil. His father advanced towards his mother, and she rushed to the kitchen, shouting. And then fury took hold and she grabbed a knife from the counter and raised her hand on a scream…

Sherry swayed, and Adrian caught her close. "Are you okay?"

She took in a breath, feeling nauseated. "We've got to go back."

"Have you forgotten something?"

"No, you need to go home, now," she said urgently. "Please trust me, Adrian."

"But why? I don't understand."

They were standing in the middle of the street and people were beginning to stare. "Something bad is going to happen at your home if we don't get there, Adrian. I need you to listen to me." She grabbed his arm and walked him briskly to his car. They'd only known each other a few weeks, and he didn't know about her gift. Not many did. How could she begin to explain what she felt? What God revealed to her? Would he even understand?

They drove in silence all the way there, and she took a moment to pray. They still had time, but he needed to hurry.

When he pulled up and parked, his father's car was already in the drive. She hoped they weren't too late. Adrian really needed to make haste. It was no longer a negotiation.

"I don't know what this is about—"

"Adrian! You must go in, now.*"*

He looked at her bewildered for a moment, then stepped out and walked to the door. Then she saw him bolt and frantically fumble with his keys to get in. She could hear the raised voices, so no doubt he could hear them too.

Squeezing her eyes shut, she continued to pray. She didn't want to see them, the way they fed off anger. If only people understood what really happened when their hearts were filled with anger.

Adrian was in there a long time, and when he finally returned, he looked distraught. His clothes were dishevelled, and his shirt was torn. Did he get into a fight with his father?

He climbed in the car but said nothing for a moment, seeming to try and compose himself. When he finally turned to her, his eyes were bleak. "How did you know?" Tears formed in his eyes and began rolling down his face.

She reached out, drawing him into her arms as he cried for his parents. For what was and would no longer be for his mother and father.

* * *

Sherry looked at the new designs for their website and assessed each and every one in detail. Shane Kinderman was head of marketing, and she couldn't find fault with his work or his team. She was always pleased with his work and he hadn't missed anything from her instructions. Responding to his email she thanked him, he'd delivered everything she'd asked for and more. She was growing to appreciate his support.

He was a nice guy, not bad to look at either, and had become a little more attentive recently. Not that she was interested or anything, but he'd definitely become more considerate: making her cups of tea during the day or turning up at her office door with lunch, and at the last team meeting, she'd seen the interest in his eyes as he watched her walk around the board room conference table.

While *he* might be interested and was pleasant enough, the problem was, she only had one man in her heart, and she didn't know how to eradicate him.

She glanced out the window. Darkness had fallen, nothing evident could be seen. She liked to look at the clouds as the plane ascended; it made her feel closer to God. But she'd missed it, becoming lost in work. She sighed and pulled down the blind.

Candace was asleep, finally. She hated being confined to such a small space, and they were both grateful that the seat between them was vacant, allowing them room to spread out a little. Sherry was used to first class, as she didn't like being squashed up around people in an enclosed space, but Candace couldn't afford first class, so they'd had no choice. As a compromise, Sherry had booked the exit-row seats so no one sat in front of them.

Already she could feel the presence behind her. She felt a chill and then an awareness. She knew then it was to be one of those moments when the Holy

Spirit would reveal His wonders, and she would be obedient to Him. She realised she was making the dark spirit uncomfortable and agitated, and this was manifested through an argument between a woman and a flight attendant. The woman began to shout, and another flight attendant rushed forward to try to control the situation as the woman stood, pointing her finger in annoyance at the attendant.

So Sherry prayed for a moment, allowing God to do His thing. She glanced down the aisle and then up; there were heavenly hosts here, four hovering above her, high above the cabin. A brilliant light shone from them, and their wings spanned the entire roof of the cabin. She was thankful there were so many, and realised belatedly that God's purpose here far exceeded normal circumstances. It wasn't usual to have so many angels on the plane. Still, she wouldn't question it. She was just content in the knowledge that she had His protection with her always. She need not fear.

She continued to pray, thanking God for his mercies and grace, and felt the angels draw nearer. Then, in answer, an uneasiness swept over her, and she looked to her left. There was a man seated in between a woman and another man. He was reading a book, his thick-rimmed glasses perched on his nose and his blonde, wispy hair thinning at the front. The first thing she noticed that was odd was the frown and perspiration at his brow, his pale complexion and the strain at his mouth. There was also a glow around him that signalled to Sherry that this man was important—*God was at work.*

"Pray for him, Sherry."

Sherry did as she was told and prayed in tongues, then waited. She faced the front again, not wanting to make it obvious she was staring. Moments drifted by where she felt the dark spirit shift and take hold. She couldn't see it, but she felt the oppression.

She looked at the man again. He began loosening his tie and his pallor had become sickly, almost grey. The woman beside him—Sherry assumed it was his wife—was asking if he was all right, and then he began to choke and seemed to have difficulty breathing, his hands clutching at his chest.

"Help! Someone please help!" his wife shouted.

By now the man was slumped in his seat, no longer conscious. The man beside him stood just as two flight attendants and two other men crowded around. "I'm a doctor," one said. "I am too," said the other. Sherry's line of sight was obscured as another two attendants gathered around to attend to the man.

She continued praying for the man's life as staff rushed back and forth. The angels also gathered around, and then she felt the atmosphere lift. She saw one of the angels reach down, she assumed to touch the man, because the next thing she heard was: "Oh, thank God! He's okay, he's okay!"

Thank God indeed. There was a round of applause from the passengers for the two doctors that had helped save that man's life, but the true gratitude needed to go to Jesus, ensuring there were not only one, but two doctors on the plane. Sherry hoped the couple would truly give thanks to God for what He had done today.

Thank you, Holy Spirit, she whispered within.

"Thank you, Sherry."

She smiled and looked over at Candace as she shifted slightly in her sleep. She was a heavy sleeper and wasn't disturbed by the commotion. Candace was silent; there was the occasional sound of deep breathing and the release of a sigh, as if she was dreaming of something good and comforting.

Sherry reached across and touched her arm. She felt her. Candace was content. Comfortable with her life and everything God had blessed her with. Sherry was pleased. There had been a time when things in Candace's life were not so pleasant. She didn't want her friend to be sad and despondent, as she'd been over her marriage breakup. It had changed her; she used to be a little more carefree about life. Sometimes there was a hint of that sadness in Candace's eyes that Sherry would try to dispel quickly with humour or some trivial anecdote, not wanting to dwell on it. But Sherry knew and in some ways understood the place they both found themselves in, a part of them still wanting men they could no longer have.

Candace was Sherry's best friend, had been since they met in business economics class at university. And then Candace met Malcolm and Sherry met

Adrian, and their relationship was less close. Then after, Sherry considered Adrian to be her best friend, and then he wasn't, and she had to adjust to what seemed to her to be a life-altering existence that tore her apart. And when she had nothing else, she sought God and deepened her relationship with Him.

Sherry prayed for Candace, laying both her hands upon her arm. As Sherry continued to pray, light penetrated her spirit and the anointing poured out of her. All the love she felt for her friend swelled inside her, touching Candace, and bringing with it healing and a blessing.

Lord, I pray that you give Candace her heart's desire, help her to find love again—let your will be done. In Jesus' name.

Sherry resumed typing, then finished the report. She tried to fight the heaviness in her eyes, but gave in. She was tired. She hadn't had much sleep.

Packing away her laptop, she adjusted the seat, and settled back to get a couple of hours' sleep, allowing her mind to drift into a dream…

They were married, and had two girls. One was eight and the other six. They were having breakfast together.

Adrian was reading the newspaper. "Come and join us at the table. You've been slaving away at the stove all morning."

"I know, but with your sister-in-law and family coming, I want to give a good impression. I can't have her thinking I can't cook."

"But you can't," he said, completely deadpan.

She laughed and hit him playfully on the shoulder. "Okay, so I made a few blunders recently, but I'm learning. I'm not really domesticated."

He pulled her on his lap, and she wrapped her arms around his neck. "You're perfect just the way you are," he said, his eyes filled with love.

Sherry touched his face and smiled. She adored this man. No matter what her failings were, he loved her regardless.

"You make awesome pancakes!" one of the girls said.

"Yes, and I like my eggs. They're all fluffy, like clouds." The little one beamed with pleasure, and Sherry was pleased she'd made her smile today. Yesterday wasn't such a good day, but they were making progress…

"Do you want a drink, Sherry?"

Sherry was jolted out of her dream. Two pairs of eyes were staring at her, waiting for a response. The flight attendant handed Candace a drink and some pretzels. Candace handed Sherry a packet.

"Yes, please. Tomato juice, thanks." Sherry yawned and ran a hand over her face.

The flight attendant looked bored. Her nametag seemed to glint in the light against her red uniform, and with Sherry's tired eyes, she was probably seeing things. Her name was Emily, her face heavily made up, her hair neatly pulled back under her red hat as she hurriedly poured drinks and handed them to passengers. Her colleague looked equally filled with boredom, her face just as made up but not as elegant as her co-worker. Her name was Hannah. Sherry had always loved that name. If she'd had children, she would have named her daughter Hannah.

Sherry sat up into a more comfortable position and lifted the blind, staring out unseeingly through the cabin window. As dawn began to break, she retraced her dream in her mind. She'd had that dream before, but it was always interrupted, and she never discovered what happened the day before and why it wasn't such a good day. She'd asked the Holy Spirit to provide the answer, but it was never revealed. She couldn't remember the girls' names, either.

She'd often wondered why God sent her the dream. It didn't make sense to her. If she was supposed to be married and have two children, then that would have happened by now. So she could only assume this was something that would have happened in the past if she hadn't gone away, and she would forever regret her decision. It had been foolish, but she couldn't take it back.

"You're quiet," Candace remarked.

Sherry looked at her. "I'm just tired. I didn't get a lot of sleep last night."

Candace took the juice from the flight attendant and handed it to Sherry. "Working, no doubt."

"No, I had to pack and then couldn't sleep for some reason." *Something's up.* She could feel it within her spirit.

"Everything at work will be fine. They can manage without you." Candace opened the pretzels and popped a few in her mouth.

It wasn't work. It was something else that Sherry couldn't quite work out. "I hope so."

"How is your father now?"

"He's okay. Strong as an ox and loves to boss me about." Sherry smiled and pulled out a cardigan from her bag. It had become decidedly chilly all of a sudden. "After this trip, I have to go and see him."

"I don't know how you do it, travelling back and forth between the US and the UK. Why haven't you settled over there? It can't be easy managing the business from the UK."

"I can do most things from our offices in London. I have a good team. My presence isn't needed in Atlanta every day." Sherry handed Candace her pretzels. She would stick to her tomato juice. She needed to lose those extra pounds she'd gained. "England is my home, plus I get the joy of both worlds. I have no one waiting for me at home, so it's okay."

"Only Lyle."

"Ha! He's not waiting for me. He's living his life. Trust me." Sherry sipped her juice.

Candace looked unconvinced and reached for the book she'd taken out of her handbag. "What are you going to do about finding Mr Right?"

"I doubt I'll find that again. I have the love of my friends and family. If God chooses to bless me with another Mr Right, then I'm open to it, but right now, I'm going to enjoy my holiday with my friend, and she's going to help me endure Marcie's wedding." Sherry slipped on her cardigan and took out her laptop, sensing a shift in the ambience again.

"Tell me about it. You know it's going to be pure extravagance."

Sherry rolled her eyes. "Yes, I'm dreading it."

<u>4</u>

There was no one closer to her than Adrian. They were so in tune that he would often know what she was thinking, and she, in turn, understood his thoughts. His favourite colour was blue. She knew this because when they were out shopping, he would always pick a blue dress or an outfit and say that would look best on her in preference to any other colour.

'My whole wardrobe can't be blue, Adrian,' she'd told him.

He grinned. 'But you'd look mighty fine, though.'

Sherry laughed and hugged him. 'You're silly.'

'Let me buy it for you.'

'You don't have to do that,' she said, still astounded at his generosity. He was always buying her things.

She also knew his moods. He rarely got angry, but when he did, it was bad. She'd only ever seen him angry twice: that night with his father, and the other with his cousin. Gary worked with him. He was always at Adrian's home, or Gary would call him often as they had a partnership of sorts.

She'd finished work for the day and arrived at his. When he opened the door, he was on the phone, and the conversation he was having with Gary seemed heated. Something about the books and payments. But what was more apparent was the presence in the room.

A dark spirit was in his office standing over his desk.

Adrian's home always had a good feel about it. It was spacious and airy. Thankfully, he didn't like clutter. The decor was masculine, and his office was neat, although it could be untidy at times, as he often had his books, folders, and invoices out open on his desk and on the floor. But never before had there been a presence here. Concerned, she began to pray and took authority over the situation. She wouldn't allow this to continue.

"What do you mean you borrowed it?" Adrian listened for a moment and began to pace. "You had better get over here and explain yourself!" He disconnected and threw the phone on his desk.

Sherry stood in front of him. "What's wrong, Adrian?"

"Gary's been stealing. And then he has the audacity to say he 'borrowed' the money!" He ran a hand through his hair; his body was rigid with tension.

She moved closer. She needed to calm him down. "How bad is it?"

"He's stolen five thousand pounds last month and another four thousand this month. I asked him about it last month and he lied, telling me some cock-and-bull story. Who knows how much he's taken over how many months—"

The doorbell sounded, and before she could do anything to stop him, Adrian was at the door, swinging it open, then Adrian had Gary pinned by the neck against the wall.

She screamed, "Adrian! Please don't do this. Come on, we'll work this out."

"I'm sorry, man… I'm sorry." Gary choked, barely able to breathe as Adrian had him held securely at his throat.

"How could you do this? After all I've done for you!" Adrian shouted.

The dark spirit appeared at Adrian's side and whispered something in his ear. Adrian tightened his hold on Gary's neck.

Lord Jesus, please intervene. *She had to do something. She grabbed Adrian's arm, but it was solid, like iron. It wouldn't budge.*

"Stay back, Sherry! This has nothing to do with you." Adrian bit out.

Cupping his face, she tried to put his focus on her. She knew that if she didn't calm him down, things would take a serious turn for the worse.

Adrian flinched. "What are you doing?"

She kissed him and whispered, "I love you, Adrian, and Jesus loves you too." She kissed his neck as he refused to take his eyes off Gary. She kissed him again and again. On his neck, his cheek, his jaw. "I love you."

"Sherry…" He glanced at her with a puzzled expression.

Gently, she kissed his lips, which caught him off guard. Then she cupped his face again, and he released his hold on Gary's throat. She took the opportunity to wrap her arms around Adrian's neck and held on tightly. "Please don't do this. Please, baby." She figured she would hold on to him for as long as it took for him to calm down.

Sherry could hear Gary coughing beside them, and when Adrian's arms slipped around her waist, she knew half the battle was won. She eased back to look at Adrian and touched his face. "Please, baby, don't do this." She caressed his cheek.

He sighed, and she felt his anger lessen. She looked down at Gary, who was bent over, rubbing his neck.

She returned her gaze to Adrian and cupped his face again. "You're better than this," she whispered. He held her gaze for a moment, and she saw a mix of emotions cross his face.

"I'm sorry," Gary said, straightening. He was of a similar build to Adrian, but was a quiet soul. She'd never picked up anything significant about him. He was in trousers and a shirt that was crumpled where Adrian had grabbed him.

"Why would you do something like this? I've given you everything. All you had to do was ask," Adrian said, his tone strained.

Tears came to Gary's eyes, and she realised then that it might be a little more serious than she'd first thought, so she drew away from Adrian's arms, knowing they would need some space to talk.

She looked for the spirit, but it had disappeared. The threat was gone. "I'll go and make us something to eat," she said, walking away, content that they would be able to work things out between them.

* * *

After waiting half an hour for the transfer service to arrive to take them to the hotel, they were shown to a meeting area outside, where the driver was waiting patiently, holding up a sign with their names. He looked hot and uncomfortable dressed in a suit. It was no wonder; the temperature was sweltering.

Sherry removed her cardigan and got into the car, grateful for the cool blast of the air conditioning. To prepare for the heat, she'd dressed light in white linen trousers, a coral pleated spaghetti top and open-toed sandals. The bright colours made her feel energised and right at home in the Caribbean.

As they settled back in the seat, she took in the beautiful greenery of Montego Bay, the sea, hills, and mountains in the distance. It was such a special place.

"So weh you ladies travelling from?" the driver asked in a Jamaican accent.

"England," Candace replied.

"Ahh, Englan.' Me have family back dere. It's nice dere, nice."

Candace looked over at Sherry and grinned. Sherry couldn't help but grin too.

The driver proceeded to talk nonstop, about the local hangouts, the best attractions, and restaurants. By the time he pulled up at the hotel, Sherry just wanted the peace and quiet of the hotel room. The huge white structure loomed ahead of them, modern and clean.

She looked out the window, and the first thing she noticed was the angel standing by the entrance to the hotel. He was dressed in translucent white robes and seemed to be waiting for something. Sherry went to open the car door, but Candace said, "Wait! We're at the wrong hotel." She looked through her paperwork.

Sherry looked at the angel again, and then two girls came running out of the reception doors chasing each other. She felt the hairs on the back of her neck stand on end, and her heart leapt. They looked like the girls from her dream!

Is he here?

Before she even thought about what she was doing, she was stepping out of the car. She vaguely heard Candace calling her name, but Sherry followed the girls in earnest, her heart pounding in her chest, looking for *Adrian.*

She followed them around the side to the pool area that led to the beach. It was packed with guests, sunbathing, swimming, and drinking by the bar.

Where is he, Lord? Please show me.

The girls ran towards a woman in a white bikini who was sunbathing near the pool. She was slim, with an enviable, model-like figure. Her long, dark hair was swept up into a bun, and dark glasses shaded her eyes.

Disappointed, Sherry felt pain sear her soul. Had she made a mistake? No, she'd seen the angel. There was a reason why the driver had stopped at this hotel. It wasn't a mistake.

She continued to watch the girls for a moment, trying to make out their faces, and then she heard footsteps running behind her.

"Sherry, what's going on?" Candace asked breathlessly when she caught up. She rested her hand on Sherry's shoulder, leaning on her heavily.

"Nothing. I thought I saw someone I know."

"I'm puffed out." Candace rested a hand on her hip. "I feel like I'm going to have a heart attack! I need to sit down."

Sherry laughed. "You're so out of shape. You need to join me in the gym while we're here."

"Yes, if we ever get to the hotel! That driver was chatting so much that he wasn't watching where he was going."

"No, I think he was supposed to stop here. Don't ask me why I think that, but I know."

Why did you bring me here, Lord?

"You must pray, Sherry."

<u>5</u>

She told him about her gift the night he gave his heart to the Lord. She'd been praying for it for so long, and God finally answered. It was a wonderful and glorious day. Adrian was fascinated with her gift and wanted to understand it. Sherry told him she didn't understand it either, only that she'd developed a relationship with the Holy Spirit, and He showed her things, but only if it was His will to do so.

Adrian believed in God and had attended church with his parents as a child, but they'd stopped attending, and thereafter was the demise of their marriage. Adrian didn't like to talk about his parent's breakup, but he did that night.

"What did you see that evening?"

He didn't need to give any further explanation. She knew what evening he was referring to, as every time she'd tried to talk to him about it, he'd shut her down. So she told him everything, even the parts that he would never have seen.

"Who started the argument?"

"Your mother," she said without hesitation and the reason God wanted her to share what she saw that night.

He looked at her then, surprised. "My mother?"

"Yes, she was provoking your father."

"But he was drunk."

"Yes, I couldn't fully understand what the argument was about. My gift allows me to see but also feel, and sometimes what I feel outweighs what I see and can be at times, more powerful." She paused and waited for him to acknowledge he understood then continued. "She seemed to be taunting him about something. The presence in the room was there before your father arrived. They thrive on strife, anger, bitterness, and resentment. There was everything in that room that night."

He was looking forward now, staring out the windscreen. He'd pulled up and parked outside her home. She looked up and could see the curtains twitch—her mother, no doubt.

She broached the subject again. Maybe this time he would answer. "What happened?"

He sighed. "I saw my father grab my mother, holding her arms around her back. I saw the knife on the floor and straight away assumed my father was trying to hurt my mother, but based on what you've told me, it was my mother all along. They argued for years. There was no love lost between them." He looked at her again. "My father and I fought that night. And from what you've said, you've confirmed his story—he's always insisted he was trying to defend himself. I never believed him because he was drunk more times than he was sober. When I went to visit him in hospital, he told me he wanted to confess all his sins and ask for forgiveness. He wants to make his life right with God before he dies."

"How much longer has he got left?"

"They don't know. Years of drinking has damaged his liver so badly it's beyond repair. He's on the waiting list for a donor, but they don't see him getting one in time. He asked for my forgiveness and told me to look after my mother." Tears came to his eyes, and he gave a big sigh, his shoulders slumped in defeat. *"I don't want him to die, Sherry. I don't want to be responsible for his business, the estate and everything. I want to live my life with you."*

She felt a sudden chill at his words. What did he mean? "I want to live my life with you." *Did that mean they couldn't be together if his father died? She took his hand.* "And we will. We'll do it together. I'll help you, Adrian. We have God. Let's pray for healing for your father. Maybe it's not too late."

"Do you think so?"

"If God wills it."

"What if He doesn't?"

She saw the fear in his eyes at the question, but didn't have an answer, so she took his other hand and led him in prayer.

* * *

"Peace, at last." Candace lay back against the bed and kicked off her shoes.

"Yes, I'm glad we've arrived, *finally*," Sherry said. After they checked in, they'd wandered around the hotel and walked down to the beach. It was a lovely hotel and was the venue for Marcie's wedding. There were four pools and Jacuzzis, and the beach stretched for miles. It was wonderful, but Sherry wanted to go off on her own to pray, though it didn't look like that was going to happen. Candace was already making plans for their evening. "I'm going to unpack some of my things and take a shower," Sherry said, and headed to her room.

They had a two-bedroom suite with a living area and kitchenette. Not that they needed a kitchen. She certainly wouldn't be cooking anything—it definitely wasn't her forte and would be room service all the way for her.

"Don't take too long. We have to go and get dinner, then I want us to go dancing…"

Dancing? Sherry wanted to eat and then roll into bed. The wedding was the following day, and she needed an early night.

The first thing she did was to pray and invited the Holy Spirit in, then she anointed the room with oil, making it holy unto the Lord. She felt His presence, and the blanket of joy that wrapped around her was warm and comforting, akin to nothing in this world.

As she undressed and stepped out of her underwear, she wondered at the mistaken trip to the hotel and the girls from her dream. For the life of her she couldn't remember their names, no matter how many times she tried to replay that part in her dream. But then, she didn't remember ever mentioning them by name. The focus had been Adrian. And then she realised for the first time since having the dreams that the girls were Adrian's children, not hers, and a sadness filled her. Then she wondered about the vision she'd been shown,

Adrian had a baby boy... Sherry could only assume it was something that would happen in the future.

She stepped in the shower, turning the temperature down, allowing the cool, powerful jets of water to cascade across her body. She relaxed and began to pray in tongues. She wanted answers.

Is he here, Lord? In Jamaica?

"Yes, Sherry. He is."

* * *

Sherry paced her bedroom floor. She was cramming for her exams. It just wasn't going in. Governance structure, financial economics, environmental reporting… Words rolled around in her head, but none of it made any sense.

Lord, please help me. I have to pass this exam.

She sipped from a bottle of water and noted the time, eight fifteen p.m. She'd been at it for ten hours straight, and she was so tired and hungry.

Her phone buzzed on the table. She picked it up.

How's it going?

She smiled at the text from Adrian. Well…it's going. I miss you. *She responded.*

While they were studying for their exams, they'd lessened the time they saw each other to once a week to focus. She missed him so much and desperately wanted to break their arrangement. She'd spent most of the day thinking about him and how terribly she missed him rather than actually studying.

I miss you too. Open your door.

Why?

Just open it.

She grinned and rushed to the window. He was standing outside. She waved like an excited schoolgirl then ran downstairs, opened the door, and flung her arms around his neck.

He held her tightly for a moment. She could tell he'd missed her just as badly as she'd missed him. She eased back and looked at him.

"I brought you dinner." He held up a bag from her favourite restaurant. She could smell the aroma of Thai chicken curry.

She hugged him again. "Ahh, Adrian, that's so sweet."

"I knew you wouldn't have eaten. And I know for definite you wouldn't have cooked. You need to feed the brain."

That was so true, she'd forgotten. It was probably why she couldn't take anything in. Grinning, she took her meal from him. "Thank you for looking after me," she said, and kissed him on the cheek.

"I love you, Sherry."

"I love you too, Adrian, always."

<u>**6**</u>

She had another sleepless night, tossing and turning, thinking about possibilities, thinking about what she would say to him.

He was married now, so there were no longer any *possibilities*, but they hadn't ended on good terms, so maybe they needed to talk and finally close the door on their relationship. Then she would be able to move forward with her life without him being forever in her heart.

But what would she say to him?

She'd thought about that moment many times over the years, but now she was at a loss.

Sherry reached for her phone in the darkness and tapped the display. It was three a.m., too early for her to be up, although in the UK it was nine in the morning. Her internal clock had not adjusted yet.

Falling back against the pillows, she stared up at the ceiling, thinking she might as well get up. But figured she'd better try to sleep, otherwise she risked having dark circles under her eyes, and wanted to ensure she looked good for the wedding.

Shifting to a more comfortable position, her mind wandered to earlier. Now that she had confirmation from the Holy Spirit that Adrian was here, she knew for definite the children were his. Was that his wife that the girls were with? She was very attractive and young. She looked to be in her late twenties or early thirties.

It made her feel inadequate. Sherry had aged since Adrian had seen her last. He probably wouldn't find her attractive anymore, especially having a wife who looked like a model. The thought embarrassed her; it wasn't as if she wanted to catch his eye or anything. He was married now, after all. But it didn't stop her from wondering about it, and it was important that she looked stunning tomorrow.

Sherry was past the age of ever being that slim again, not that she wanted to be. Training every day meant that when she put on weight, it wasn't the end of the world. She'd long since accepted the changes in her body, and some things she couldn't go back to. Like eating like a bird. Those days were *over*. As long as she fit comfortably in clothes and kept firm, she was content with that.

So why was she comparing herself to his wife?

If she was truly honest with herself, she'd say that she always wondered if Genevieve was prettier than she was, and if that had been the reason Adrian chose Genevieve over her. That was her name— *Genevieve*—she'd thought it was the most quintessential name of stature and represented her standing in society. Having seen Genevieve at the hotel, Sherry could see that she clearly was the complete, perfect package; there was no way Sherry could ever have competed with her.

Sherry sighed.

Lord, is he happy?

She genuinely hoped he was. It was all she'd ever wanted for him. But she somehow sensed he wasn't. Over the years when she'd asked about him, some things God would not reveal to her. She couldn't help but think about him and wonder. It made her feel unsettled to know that he could possibly be unhappy.

Adrian had always been so caring and loving towards her. She loved the sunshine in his smile, and she'd fallen for him deeply. He was one of those men that she would call *brotherly*, having all those wonderful attributes, kind-hearted and gentle—compassionate and sensitive. At twenty-three, he'd known who he was and what he wanted in life. He was so much more mature than their friends, confident in his values, and would not deviate from them. In upholding those views, he treated her as though she were a precious jewel that he handled with the utmost care. Never once had he ever spoken badly to her, which had inadvertently spoiled her for anyone else. Even his smiles and the way he looked at her at times seemed only for her, and it was no wonder that she fell for him. He went out of his way to take care of her and just love her. He was sweet, too, one of those guys who women took advantage of. She had no misgivings in guarding and protecting him from others who might try to take advantage of him.

There were little things that she'd also taken for granted, things that she thought, like a fool, that all men in love would be like. He always had an affectionate way with her. He enfolded her in his arms and kissed her often. She'd never experienced it with anyone else. She mistakenly thought all men were the same in that regard, but it was so far from the truth.

She'd been blessed to have him.

Sherry remembered times when she would forget breakfast or lunch, and he made a point to ensure she ate healthily. Some evenings when they spent time at his, he would cook, experimenting with recipes from a thirty-minute cookbook she'd bought for him as a present. Meals with him had become all the more special because he made their meals from scratch. They would have romantic dinners by candlelight and stare into each other's eyes and talk about how wonderful it was going to be when they got married.

She pictured him one night as he reached across the table for her hand, his gaze locked with hers, and said, *"There is no other place I want to be than with you, Sherry."*

And she had always felt the same way. Life without him had been difficult, and all she had were memories of a man who was so young, yet was always so mature and a true gentleman.

There was no one like Adrian. She recalled the very first time he'd made her feel special. Her mind flashed to the past and she closed her eyes at the pain she still felt at not having him in her life.

* * *

Her lectures had finished for the day and he was waiting for her outside. He wore jeans and a t-shirt, showing off his broad chest and strong, muscular arms. The weather was warm with a gentle breeze, and she was thankful she'd made more of an effort that morning, deciding on a summer dress and sandals. She could honestly say she looked pretty in her yellow polka dot tea dress.

Despite herself, she grinned, as she hadn't expected him to be interested in her. She'd seen the girls he went for, and she wasn't his type. She knew they would be friends, but from the look in his eyes, he was definitely *interested in a whole lot more.*

"Are you going home?"

"Yes, I've got a mock exam tomorrow."

He reached over and gently removed her handbag and book bag from her shoulder. She wondered what he was doing and stared at him.

"Let me take your bags. They're heavy."

Astounded, she continued to stare for a moment. She'd never had a man do that for her. Most guys she dated had been quite immature and they never evolved any further than friendships. "You don't need to do that."

He took the bags from her. "I want to."

"Thank you," she said, and smiled as they made their way down the street, dodging the milling students talking in groups.

"Do you need any help with the mock?"

"Can you sit the exam for me?" She was being facetious, but wanted to see what reaction she would get.

"I could help you, and you could help me." He smiled, and she felt weak at the knees.

She doubted he needed help. He was intelligent and excelling in class, and was one of the top students amongst his peers. So was she, but the difference was, she had to work at it.

He walked her back to her place. She shared a house with five other students. She was grateful they were not home as yet, otherwise they would have appeared and caused a nuisance, no doubt fawning all over him. She'd seen them in action around guys on campus.

As they approached her door, he reached over, gently took her keys from her, and opened the door. She giggled.

"What's so funny?"

"Oh, nothing."

He looked at her and raised a brow.

"I've never had anyone do that before, take my bags and carry them, then take my keys and open the door."

"You're a special lady, Sherry. So you should be treated that way." His eyes were warm and assessing.

She smiled and felt heat blush her cheeks. He made her feel so… "Did you want to come in?" she offered.

"No, I just wanted to look at you for a while and talk to you." He handed her bags back to her and then kissed her on the cheek.

"I'll call you, Sherry," he said, looking deep into her eyes, and then he winked.

Instantly smitten, she wanted to follow when he walked away. As she turned, closing the door behind her, she smiled to herself and hoped that he walked her home tomorrow.

7

"I love you, Lord," she whispered.

"I love you too, Sherry."

Turning in bed, she listened to the whispers in her heart against the beautiful sounds she could hear from outside her hotel room. They had fantastic views of the beach and the ocean. Her room had a balcony; she'd ensured that.

After a few hours of tossing and turning, she'd eventually drifted off to sleep again with thoughts of Adrian, but with a renewed wish.

Rising from the bed, Sherry stretched, then tiptoed to the balcony and gently opened the sliding doors, not wanting to disturb Candace in the adjacent room. The welcoming cool breeze fluttered her nightdress, and then the warmth of the sun hit her skin. It was going to be a hot day today.

She began to pray in tongues as she watched the water flow in and out onto the beach. It was such a majestic sight. She loved it here, in Jamaica. The beach was empty, as it was still early. She could hear birdsong in the distance, and the sounds from the sea were therapeutic and calming.

Taking a seat in one of the balcony chairs, she delighted in the light show of the sunrise, the golden sun bursting through with yellows, oranges, and reds. It was so, so beautiful. She was filled with awe at the splendour of God's creation.

You did this, Lord. You created such a wonderful and beautiful earth. Thank you. I will never fail to be delighted at your creation.

She smiled as she heard Him chuckle.

"And I delight in you, Sherry, my love," Holy Spirit said.

Tears came to her eyes at his words.

"There are a few things I want to show you today. Be alert and aware of me. You must pray and be vigilant. I am with you, always. Delight in me."

She felt a sweeping sense of unease touch her spirit and didn't know why. *What is it, Lord?*

"Pray, Sherry."

Then she asked, because Adrian was never far from her thoughts, *Is he here, Lord? At the hotel?*

"Yes."

Her heart leapt and a desperate need to see him filled her. All the love she felt for him suffused her heart.

"Stay focused, Sherry. I am with you."

While she continued to pray, she wondered at the Holy Spirit's words. She knew He was always with her. Why had He told her that? She felt again that tinge of unease that settled within her spirit, but was obedient and prayed, for something was surely going to happen today, something that needed to be guarded against. Was it to do with Adrian?

She waited to see if the Holy Spirit would answer, but all she heard was the whisper of the wind from the shore.

An hour later, when the sun and all its splendour took centre stage and she felt a release to cease prayer for a moment, the buzz of her phone alerted her to a message.

She glanced at it. Angela.

Smiling, she reached for the mobile and swiped to reveal Angela's message.

I love you.

Sherry's smile broadened. She messaged back, her heart swelling with love for her sister. *I love you too, Angie. I miss you.*

I'm missing you too. When are you back?

Next Friday, and you had better have dinner ready, because you know I won't be cooking.

Haha, yes! Don't I know it. Enjoy the wedding and send lots of photos.

I will.

Sherry returned the phone to the table, thinking about her family. She missed them. She knew her mother would message next. She never failed to keep in contact, which Sherry was grateful for. Her life became busy at times, and her mother would be a gentle reminder of her roots and home.

She recalled the last time she was there for dinner.

Mum was in the kitchen and her husband, Colin, was in the living room watching football. Colin was nice, though he wasn't as good looking or as commanding as her father. He was average height with a tawny skin tone, a little out of shape, and on the heavier side. Her father would never have let himself go like that. It made Sherry wonder at her mother's attraction. Granted, Colin was a nice person, and he treated her mother well, but it had taken a while to get used to him, as a small part of her secretly wanted her parents to get back together. She'd even tried inviting her mother to visit Atlanta a few times, but she refused, and Sherry didn't fully understand why.

'Do you need any help, Mum?'

'Help to cook? Yeah right, Sherry.'

'Haha Mother, I can peel potatoes or cut onions competently.'

Mum laughed, *'Okay, you know where they are.'*

Sherry smiled and bent to retrieve a handful of potatoes from one of the lower cupboards, then selected a knife from the cutlery drawer and began the tedious task of peeling potatoes, one of her pet hates.

'How is your father?' Mum asked, her tone slightly lowered, Sherry suspected her mother didn't want Colin to overhear.

She wondered at that, and often felt a vibe between them. Not wanting to pry, she didn't dwell on it, just prayed for them at a distance. If her mother wanted her intervention, she would ask. Ordinarily they seemed happy, so she didn't focus on it, but there was something…

'He's good—stronger.' Sherry smiled. *'He's attending church now.'*

Mum stopped stirring the sauce and looked at her *'He's attending church?'*

'Yes, and making a stir with the ladies.' The last part Sherry added to see what reaction she would get. After Mum and Dad divorced, Mum had since remarried. Her parents refused to tell her what happened between them. Every time she asked, she got the standard response: *'Oh I don't want to talk about the past.'* Both her parents failed to address the fact that their past fed their future.

'He's seeing someone?'

'Well…he's dating again. I'm pleased for him." Sherry looked at her mother closely. *'You seem surprised.'*

'I guess I am.' Mum said with a contemplative expression.

'Why did you two break up?'

'Because he stopped going to church, he stopped believing and became angry at life.'

There was a look in her mother's eyes. It was there for only a moment, and as if it were a stage play that had been practiced and performed many times, Colin made an appearance like he'd been listening in the wings.

He stood close and wrapped his arms around her waist. *'What are you cooking, sweetheart?'*

Colin always called her that, which was sweet. Mum loved it too, as her eyes would light up with love.

Mum turned to him. *'Duck à l'orange, your favourite.'*

'You know how to please your man.' he said, as if it was a declaration of his claim on her. He gave Mum a quick kiss and rummaged in the fridge, and Sherry wondered at that and if there was some distrust and insecurities between them, but before she could contemplate it any further, the doorbell sounded and Colin was making his way to open the door. Angela had arrived.

Sherry dropped the potato and the knife in the sink, washed and dried her hands, then walked to the hallway to greet her sister. *'Angie.'* Sherry hugged her close.

'Hey, sis.' Angie was in a snazzy halter-neck and skinny jeans, her long hair swept up into a ponytail. She had grown into a very beautiful woman. Sherry was amazed at the transformation from the shy teenager to the confident and outgoing woman Angie had become.

'Sis,' Owen said, holding out his arms, and Sherry happily stepped into them. Angela's husband was huge. Sherry got lost in his hugs. Owen was lovely and totally besotted with Angela. They were so in love. Sherry felt it between them, so strong and profound.

'Aunty Sherry!' Clad in jeans and bright t-shirts, two bundles of joy ran into her legs.

She hugged them both. *'Hi, Jessica. Hi, Robert. What did you bring for me?'*

They looked at her, then looked at each other, and Angela and Owen burst out laughing at their expressions.

'Nothing, then?' Sherry rolled her eyes.

'We'll bring you something next time, we promise.' They held out their hands in expectation of whatever gift Sherry had brought for them.

'I swear your children only love me because of the gifts I bring for them. They are soooo spoilt,' Sherry teased with a smile. They were so far from spoilt. They were the most well-behaved children she'd ever been around, and she loved them so. She was grateful she'd had a hand in raising them. The many nights of babysitting she'd done over the years had to count for something.

Sherry reached for the two carrier bags on the floor beside the table and handed them one each from her last trip to America.

They grinned. *'Thank you, Aunty Sherry!'* they said in unison.

She leaned forward to allow them to kiss her on each cheek and then run off into the living room.

As Angela and Owen went to greet Mum, Sherry shut the front door and headed for the living room to spend some time with Jessica and Robert, but before she could do that, her mother called out, *'Sherry, the potatoes are not going to peel themselves...'*

Sherry chuckled to herself as she remembered trying to get out of the domesticity of the kitchen that day. Her mother knew her so well.

She sighed, her thoughts drifting to Adrian and his wife again. She wondered for the hundredth time what she would say to him.

<u>8</u>

She hugged him excitedly. "I can't believe I found it, and the rent is really cheap."

"Don't you think it might be better to stay on at your mother's until…you know…things change?"

Sherry leaned back to look at Adrian. He hadn't officially asked her to marry him as yet. They'd touched on it briefly. It seemed to be the natural course for their lives and was what she wanted. She hoped he did too.

"I know financially it doesn't make sense, but I wanted my own space. Going back after being away at university is a little uncomfortable with Colin being there and everything. And them being newlyweds, it must be difficult for them too. The rent here is less than what I was paying at uni, and I have a few job interviews lined up, so it will be fine. Stop worrying."

They stood in the middle of what would be her living room. It was spacious, but unfurnished, so she would have to buy a sofa and a few items. Mum had said Sherry could take her bed, so she was ready to move in and looking forward to her time here in her first-floor, one-bedroom flat.

She took his hand and led him to the windows. The garden backed onto an open space of green fields and meadows, and further in the distance, horses were grazing. "Look at the views. Amazing, huh?"

Her flat was on the outskirts of London in the quiet village town of Barringswood. It wasn't the easiest to get to without a car, but once she started working, she would purchase one.

He smiled and slipped his arm around her waist, and she leaned into him. "Yes, a little piece of country. When we're married, I want us to have a place with views like this."

Sherry grinned and looked at him. "So we're getting married, then?"

"Yes, of course we are."

Her heart leapt. She tried to tamp down the excitement she felt, not wanting him to feel obligated or influenced in any way. She wanted this lifetime commitment to be something he wanted to do wholeheartedly. But despite herself, her grin broadened. "It would be so perfect to live somewhere like this. How many bedrooms will our house have?"

"Five, enough room for our children." He looked at her, his eyes intense, then he leaned in and kissed her. She closed her eyes and held on, slipping her arms around his neck, as with every kiss, the love they felt for each other engulfed her, sending her emotions into a tailspin.

After a long moment, he ended the kiss. She was giddy and filled with joy knowing how wonderful life would be when they were married.

* * *

"You look stunning," Candace remarked as Sherry made the final touches to her makeup.

Sherry decided on a blue, one-shoulder midi dress. The thin material was just bearable in the heat. Why Marcie decided to have her wedding on a beach, Sherry didn't know. While it was romantic and all that, it meant the majority of her friends couldn't attend, and the heat was *draining*. Sherry just wanted to sleep. Thank God her hair was short. Her hairdresser had convinced her to try a pixie cut, and it was the best thing she'd ever done. She wouldn't have been able to cope with long hair on and around her neck. Candace's curls had already begun to droop. Still, she looked so pretty in an apricot off-the-shoulder dress, her hair styled with a cascade of curls twisted to the side. "Thank you." Sherry smiled. "You look amazing, Candace. All the men in this place will be falling over themselves to be with you."

Candace's face lit up. "You think so?" She nudged Sherry out of the view of the mirror and looked at her length to her heels, turning left and then right. She grinned. "You're right, I *do* look amazing."

Sherry laughed, shaking her head. "You know you can't wear those heels on the sand, regardless of how beautiful they are." Candace had been proud when she bought the apricot Casadei sandals with sparkling gemstones to match her dress, but unfortunately, they were not very practical for a beach wedding. Sherry had gone for wedge open-toe sandals, which were perfect for the beach.

"Well, it's all about the look, I'll slip them off on the beach and put them back on in the hotel." Candace looked down at her feet, then back at Sherry and said, "I do have to wonder, though…"

Sherry gave one last glance in the mirror and grabbed her clutch bag. "And what is that?"

"Why you've chosen to wear blue." Candace raised an eyebrow.

"Because this colour suits me."

"Or is it because someone in particular called Adrian likes you in blue." Candace gave a teasing grin.

"I'm not going to dignify that with a response." Sherry tried to hide the smile that came to her lips.

They made their way downstairs to reception, and she couldn't help the nervous butterflies in her tummy. She hadn't been able to stop thinking about Adrian and the Holy Spirit's revelation. It meant that Adrian was attending the wedding. Why didn't Marcie tell her she'd invited Adrian? She knew they used to date. She also knew they'd intended to get married, although that was short-lived.

Sherry stopped and retrieved the fan from her handbag that she'd acquired from the hotel gift shop. "It's so hot," she said, flicking open the fan in an attempt to cool herself. She could feel a trickle of perspiration crawl down her spine. She looked up, wondering at the lack of air conditioning. All there appeared to be was old-fashioned ceiling fans in the reception area.

"I know, it's unbearable. But I love it. I could live here," Candace said, fanning herself with her hand.

"Yes, me too."

They headed to the beach and joined the other guests taking their seats lined up around the flower altar. The view was spectacular, crystal-blue waters and white sands as far as the eye could see. It was beautiful. Sherry wished she could spend some time alone on the beach, barefoot, taking in the atmosphere. It was unfortunate her day wouldn't be spent that way. She hated weddings. It was a reminder of what she could have had and had always hoped for, but would never have now.

Looking down at her hand, she fingered the engagement ring that she'd never taken off since the day Adrian had given it to her. In her heart he was her husband, no one else could ever take his place, and while that possibility was no longer an option for her, it didn't change the way she felt, and accepting that was the most difficult to endure.

She sighed and let Candace lead the way. They were early, so they took a seat in the fourth row down. Her mind drifted to fifteen years ago, when she was young and naive and so in love with Adrian.

* * *

They'd been seeing each other for a year and had planned a life together. Even down to how many children they would have. Adrian told her he would look after her. He already had a business and a lucrative income. He'd started off dabbling in the stock market, using his trust fund wisely, and then become a major shareholder in three companies. How he'd managed that at only twenty-three was beyond her. She was amazed at his intellect and wanted to learn from him. He was competitive by nature and got a buzz out of making money, sometimes being ruthless in his dealings. She would watch him sometimes while he worked, and his eyes would gleam with pleasure when he made a profit on a large scale. He seemed to enjoy the game that to many would be a considerable risk.

He'd always said he didn't want to work for anyone else, not even his parents, and he'd already achieved his goal. She sometimes got the feeling that he was trying to compete with his father and wanted to prove something.

Adrian's family were wealthy—well, his mother was now. When his father died, he'd left them enough money to keep them comfortable for the rest of their lives. Adrian had set up his business when he was nineteen, and he'd told Sherry he'd hardly touched his trust fund.

She, however, hadn't been so focused and was still looking at options for work. Adrian had told her to work with him, and she was thinking about it. The idea was becoming more appealing as time went on. The problem was, she'd fallen so deeply in love with him that he'd become everything to her, and she wanted to spend every moment with him. Her cautious side told her that maybe spending every moment with him might not be wise as they continued their relationship, but she loved being with him. There was no one else that she would rather be with.

That evening he'd taken her to see a film at Leicester Square in London, and afterwards he'd draped his arm around her shoulders as they'd taken a walk to Trafalgar Square. They crossed the large pedestrian-walk and took a seat on one of the benches under one of the lion statues.

He turned to her and gently cupped her face. "I love you, Sherry."

She smiled. "I love you too, Adrian."

"I adore you. You're everything to me, and I want us to spend the rest of our lives together." He kissed her then, so gently that it brought tears to her eyes, as well as a rush of emotion she found difficult to contain. And when he pulled away, she tucked herself into his side and closed her eyes when he wrapped his arm around her.

He fingered the ring he'd given her that she'd vowed never to take off. It was a beautiful, simple white diamond set in a gold band. She loved it—she loved him, *and wanted so much to be his wife.*

"We need to speak to our parents and begin to make plans."

"Okay, where will we live?" she asked. "We haven't really spoken about that."

"With me, of course."

His apartment was amazing. It was a three-bedroom structure on three floors with a garden, it was more like a town house, and it was perfect for the two of them until they decided to start their family. She grinned. "Okay."

* * *

"Oh, look! There's Cheryl," Candace shrieked, jolting Sherry out of her reverie. "I haven't seen her since we were at uni. Cheryl! Hi!"

Sherry watched as Cheryl walked over to them, and they stood and greeted her. "Wow! What has it been, fifteen years?" Cheryl asked. "I haven't seen either of you since."

Cheryl had always been the beautiful one that men flocked to. She was still attractive, but Sherry could see the years hadn't been kind to her. Her face was drawn and her eyes were sad. They used to be close at one time, but they'd just stopped texting each other, and Sherry didn't know why. Cheryl had married a multimillionaire, and maybe things were not as rosy as everyone thought. If Sherry was to touch her, she would know, but she didn't want to pry into Cheryl's life unless it was God's will for her to do so, and at this time it wasn't. She said a silent prayer for Cheryl.

Cheryl looked at her. "I've missed you, Sherry. Why didn't we stay in touch?"

"I don't know. Life got in the way, I guess."

Cheryl reached over to hug her, and as soon as she did that, images formed before Sherry, of hurt, pain, fear, and suppression. Cheryl was being abused by her husband.

Shocked for a moment, Sherry held on tighter. She closed her eyes and whispered a prayer over Cheryl, drawing on her anointing to bring about healing and restoration. Sherry remembered what had happened in that cave all those years ago. The enemy wanted to take her then but failed, and now he was trying to take her spirit another way.

Anger filled her. She wouldn't allow it, not anymore. She realised then that her purpose at the wedding wasn't just to put her past to bed. She was here for Cheryl, too, as she was back then. She was reminded of the Holy Spirit's words that morning. This was what he wanted to show her.

She heard a sob come from Cheryl, and Sherry eased away slightly but kept her hands on Cheryl's shoulders. God had a work to do, after all.

"I don't know why I'm crying," Cheryl said, getting a tissue from her handbag and dabbing at her tears. "I didn't realise how much I missed you."

"Let's not let another day go without talking to each other." Sherry hugged her again.

Cheryl smiled, and the sadness in her eyes disappeared. "Oh, please! I would love that."

As Cheryl reached into her handbag to retrieve her mobile to exchange numbers, Sherry recalled when she and Cheryl were close, and in love with the two men they'd planned to marry.

* * *

"A hike up mountains? You've got to be joking," Cheryl scoffed. "I'm spending the day on the beach with a good book." Cheryl proceeded to make herself comfortable on a sun lounger, removing her beach sarong to work on her tan.

"And I'm going to spend the day watching Cheryl read that book." Jeff grinned.

"Looks like it's just you and me, kiddo," Adrian said.

Sherry smiled. "Looks like it." She was pleased Cheryl and Jeff were staying behind. She wanted to spend some time alone with Adrian, and besides, Jeff and Cheryl bickered—a lot. They'd spoken of marriage, but it was too soon for them. They needed to get to know each other a little more. They were in love, there was no doubt about that, but there were doubts and insecurities that they needed to address, and maybe in some ways, Sherry and Adrian also needed to address those same insecurities.

It was the end of summer, and they'd decided to go on holiday with friends. Jamaica had been the obvious choice for the Caribbean. And so far, they'd had so much fun. They'd been out every day. Jet skiing had been crazy. They both fell off the jet skis twice. She'd been totally soaked. Thankfully, with the weather being so warm, she'd dried off pretty quick. They'd then tried their hands at horse riding along the beach, snorkelling, and dolphin watching, then cruising on a catamaran. They hadn't stopped.

After the bus ride to Blue Mountains, they spent the night at a lodge nearby and would meet up with Cheryl and Jeff for dinner when they returned the following day.

Adrian reached for Sherry's hand as they climbed upwards across the plane. The tour guide was providing interesting facts about the history of Jamaica. She couldn't say she was highly enamoured with the talk. She just couldn't stop thinking about Adrian. She was besotted, and he knew it. She wasn't ashamed of her feelings and openly expressed how she felt, and so did he.

Still, they were careful and had decided to wait until they were married, and she was thankful about that—and so were her parents. She didn't know what his *mother thought, though. She tended to be aloof and distant whenever Sherry visited and had to endure one of her dinners.*

Adrian was an only child and was close to his mother. When Sherry first met Miriam, she was pleasant. Sherry had been terrified at the prospect of meeting her. But when she did, Miriam was lovely, until she wasn't…

As soon as Miriam discovered that they intended to be married, her demeanour towards Sherry changed. It was subtle at first; she'd thought she was imagining things. When the three of them were together, Miriam appeared congenial, but when Miriam smiled or looked at Sherry, her eyes appeared cold. And then there was that time when Adrian had asked her to meet him at his mother's because he'd been stuck at work, and Miriam had been like ice.

Sherry hadn't imagined it.

"So, Sherry, what do you plan to do when you and my son get married?" Miriam asked. Her complexion was fair, attributable to her mixed-race heritage. Although she was an attractive woman, her face was heavily made up, as if she were hiding behind a mask, and her long, dark hair was pulled back severely into a bun. She wore a charcoal-grey dress and heels, personifying the ultimate ice queen who was always so formal and never relaxed in her home.

Miriam raised her eyebrow in question, then continued, not waiting for a response. "My son has worked hard with his business and needs a woman who is hardworking by his side, not someone who wants to live off him. Have you ever worked, Sherry? You're twenty-three, aren't you?"

Sherry blinked, trying to shield herself against the sting of Miriam's words. "Well, I've been studying, I hope to find a job now that university is over."

"By now I would have expected you must have some plans as to what you want to do. Do you intend to live off my son?"

Shocked at the turn in their conversation and her obvious unpleasantness and clear dislike, Sherry said nothing for a moment and discerned oppression around this woman that she'd never picked up on before. God had shown her, hadn't he? He'd shown her in that vision what was within this woman.

How had she missed this? She'd visited four times in the past, and Sherry had always been so shielded and basked in Adrian's love that she hadn't taken the time to discern as she usually did. She'd let her guard down, taking for granted that his family would love her just as he did. Besides, Miriam was close to Adrian, so surely this bitter, resentful, and hateful woman couldn't possibly produce such a warm and loving son. It didn't make sense to her. And the other thing that had become apparent was that Sherry also discerned jealousy.

Why would Miriam be jealous of me?

"Sherry, I'm sorry, but you are not the type of woman that I expected my son to marry. Your family are underprivileged, and so are you. You wouldn't fit in with us even if you tried. I want you to reconsider your plans with my son. At the moment things are new between you—he sees you as a plaything and is enamoured by you—but he will soon become bored of you. I've seen it before."

Plaything? Bored of me? What is she saying? Adrian loves me. *She watched Miriam's eyes change to amused pleasure. She enjoyed being spiteful, it would seem.*

"Did he tell you about his ex-girlfriend? He planned to marry her too." Miriam raised an eyebrow expectantly.

Adrian had told her about his past girlfriends, but he'd never mentioned one he planned to marry. Sherry's ignorance must have shown on her face, because Miriam continued on.

"He never told you? Well, that says enough. My son can be fickle at times, and reckless. I suppose he hasn't told you about Isabella either, I take it?"

Isabella?

Miriam tried to look sympathetic, but any attempt at compassion did not meet her eyes.

"The best advice I would give you would be to reconsider. Enjoy my son, spend time with him, but marriage to you would be a mistake. You're not the woman he should be with. Genevieve is."

Sherry said nothing in response and looked away. She felt tears threaten but refused to give in to them in front of this woman. All she wanted to do was pray.

"There, you see, you don't know my son as well as you thought, do you?" Miriam gave a satisfied smile, and shortly after, Adrian arrived.

He and Sherry argued that night—badly. It had been their first argument, and the very first time she'd really experienced the enemy's wiles and let him affect her. She'd allowed the door to open and did not guard herself against it and Adrian's mother.

<u>9</u>

"I heard you had children," Candace said.

"Oh, yes, I had three. They're teenagers now." Cheryl looked proud. "They're at home with my parents. My husband and I decided to come over on our own. We're only here for a couple of nights. He has to work." Cheryl swiped through pictures of her family on her phone.

They chatted for a while, and Sherry nervously looked around as more guests joined them. The hundred or so seats slowly filled up, but there was still no sign of Adrian.

Sherry began to feel impatient; she'd waited so long for this moment, yearned just to see him, and now, as she waited, making small talk with Cheryl, her heart raced out of control at the thought of finally being able to just say the things she'd held inside for so long—to the man who would have been *her husband*. The man she'd intended to have three babies with. Her heart ached at the thought, and she returned her focus on Cheryl.

Sherry observed, not feeling the need to respond as Cheryl spoke about her life. It was clear that her whole life revolved around her husband, as every sentence ended in *"my husband and I."* Sherry wondered if that would have been her fate. When she thought back, she hadn't fully decided on what she wanted to do with her career at the time Adrian had asked her to marry him, and presumably he would have wanted her to be a wife and mother. She'd wanted that life, but wholeheartedly she still wanted a career. Solely depending upon him financially had been an uncomfortable thought, to say the least.

She remembered when she finally found a job as a PA at an investment firm. She'd wondered deep down if Adrian really wanted her to have a career. She suspected he didn't. It was something they hadn't fully discussed.

* * *

They'd gone out for celebratory drinks at their local hangout—a restaurant called Madison's where they often met up with their friends. Adrian had been happy for her and hugged her along with everyone else. And when Marcie and Candace started the round of toasts and speeches to Sherry's new found career, Adrian lifted his glass, but there was something in his eyes, and Sherry wasn't sure what it was. She wanted to ask, but the evening turned into silliness and laughter, and Jeff had way too much to drink.

Much later, Cheryl felt it was a good idea to dance on a table and sing karaoke, which had the whole restaurant in an uproar, dancing and buying more rounds of drinks. When the night finally came to an end, Gary volunteered to take Jeff home.

Adrian had parked nearby. It was a short distance, so he took Sherry's hand, and they walked together in silence for a while, which was unusual for them, so she knew something was wrong.

She squeezed his hand. "What's wrong, Adrian?"

He looked at her. "What are you going to do at this job of yours?"

Job of mine? He makes it sound as if it's a passing phase. *"I'm not sure yet. I'll let you know when I start next week. I'm an assistant to one of the partners at the firm."*

"So a glorified secretary, then?"

"Not quite, Adrian." She didn't like his tone. She'd thought he was happy for her. He'd been fine when she told him over the phone.

"Isn't that the role of a personal assistant?"

She stared at him for a moment. "I thought you would be happy for me. You said you were."

"I am. I'm just trying to understand your reasoning. You have a degree in business. We've spoken about this—you planned to start your own business. You didn't want to work for anyone."

Adrian's expression was serious, his eyes holding hers as though this was important to him, but it was more than that. It was as if there was something behind it, and she wondered if it had something to do with his mother. Maybe his mother felt working for someone was beneath them. Did Adrian feel the same way?

"I don't want to work for anyone, and yes, I do intend to have my own business one day, but I need experience in the business world. It will help me form my ideas."

He stopped walking and drew her nearer to him. "But you promised you would work for me. I can teach you those things."

If she was honest with herself, the real reason she'd found this job was since that day at his mother's home, Miriam's words had been racing around Sherry's head. His mother made her feel inadequate, and she wanted to prove Miriam wrong. She was also suddenly afraid that what Miriam had said about Adrian was true, that he was fickle and their relationship may not last. Sherry didn't want to tie herself and her career to him in case things in the end didn't work out. She'd believed him when he said they would marry, but he'd asked Genevieve and Isabella too. And it worried her because he'd never said a word.

She stepped close to him and placed a hand to his chest. She could feel his hurt, and she didn't want that. "I know, and you will. I thought that maybe I could do both. This job finishes at four. I could work with you for a few hours a day, and then we can have dinner like we usually do, and I'd work full days with you at the weekend. What do you think?" He was still uneasy, but he'd relaxed a little. She stroked his chest. "Please, baby, be happy for me."

"I am, but I wanted you to work for me full-time."

"I will eventually, but I need to learn about finance and the investments market."

"I can teach you that too."

Why was he taking this personally? "And you will. I intend to learn everything from you." She touched the side of his face. "It won't be forever, and then I'll work for you full-time."

He seemed content with that, and they sealed it with a kiss. He pulled her close and slung an arm around her shoulders, and they resumed their walk to the car.

She hoped it wouldn't cause a rift between them.

* * *

Eventually, Cheryl's husband came over and Cheryl introduced them. Keith was good looking. Sherry could see why Cheryl had fallen for him. He had perfect features; clean-shaved, square-jaw, and dark eyes. Having all the attributes of a dashingly handsome man, confident and commanding, but something wasn't right. He had a presence of arrogance and conceit about him. She watched the way he possessively curled his arm around Cheryl's waist, drawing her nearer to him. Cheryl seemed to stiffen at his touch, and had what appeared to be a fake smile on her face that didn't quite reach her eyes. She wondered what had happened between Cheryl and Jeff. They'd intended on marriage and had been in love.

Was the love game so capricious? *Can you be so in love with someone, yet in the end the person that you love above all else turns out not to be the one you're with?*

It didn't make sense to Sherry, it was a mystery that had left her feeling empty and unfulfilled. She recalled when Jeff and Cheryl were together. They had their ups and downs, but they were meant to be. Why had she married this Keith? Why had Adrian married someone else, for that matter?

* * *

On their return to the hotel after the hike up Blue Mountain Peak and the long trip back, Sherry and Adrian headed out to the beach to find Jeff sprawled out, sunning himself on a lounger, his sunglasses perched on his nose, dressed in a red t-shirt and colourful striped shorts, exposing tanned, hairy legs. He, along with most of the hotel guests, had decided it was too hot now to venture out.

"Where's Cheryl?" Sherry asked. Jeff and Cheryl had been inseparable since they'd arrived at the hotel. It wasn't like her to go off on her own.

Jeff pushed his sunglasses to his forehead and looked at her. "We had an argument and she walked off in a huff." He shrugged.

Sherry hadn't been in tune before, but she felt it now, the tightness in her chest, the uneasiness. "What time was this?"

"A couple of hours ago. She likes to walk off her anger. Leave her. She'll come back when she's calmed down."

A couple of hours ago? *She looked at him in disbelief. "This isn't London, Jeff. She could be hurt, lost or something. You shouldn't have let her go off on her own."*

Adrian frowned, his expression making it clear he wasn't impressed with Jeff's response. "You shouldn't have let her go, Jeff."

"She'll be all right, I promise you." Jeff lowered his sunglasses back over his eyes and settled off to sleep.

Sherry shook her head in disgust, wanting to throttle him. Where was the care? She was thankful Adrian wasn't like that. In fact, they'd never argued. Not once. And it wasn't because he agreed with everything she said or that she agreed with him, but because they had a lot in common, and when they didn't agree, they compromised. Wasn't that how it was supposed to be in relationships? Jeff had a lot to learn when it came to women. Jeff and Adrian were so totally different in character, and she often wondered how they came to be friends.

Adrian would never have let her go off on her own. This was yet another example of how special Adrian was and how blessed she was that God had brought someone like him into her life. She still hadn't gotten over how Adrian had gently taken her coat when they'd gone out two weeks ago and taken her hand, helping her down a flight of stairs in case she fell in her high-heeled sandals. She'd grinned like the cat that had got the cream, amazed at his consideration. He was such a gentleman. Who does that? *She thought. It was a new experience for her. He made her feel loved and cared for. Adrian was one of a kind, an outlier to the norm. Still, so was she.*

Sherry looked at Adrian with concern. "I'm going to check back at the hotel."

Back at the room that she shared with Cheryl, there was no sign of her. Sherry began to worry. Where is she, Lord? Please show me.

Closing her eyes, she began to pray. She felt God's presence fill her, and a powerful light streamed into the room and seemed to embrace her. A picture was revealed, and instantly she knew where Cheryl was.

Rushing out of the hotel, she made her way out to the beach, away from the hotel, then turned right on to a trail of green foliage and fruit trees. She walked on determinedly, praying Cheryl was okay, but deep down, she knew something was wrong.

"Sherry! Hold up."

She turned to Adrian as he ran towards her.

"Hey, don't go off like that, okay?" He skimmed her arms affectionately. "I don't want anything happening to you."

"I'm sorry, I'm just concerned for Cheryl. Something's wrong."

"What makes you think there's something wrong? Jeff said she does this a lot when she's angry."

"I just know, Adrian, trust me." She walked on and came to a clearing and what looked like an opening to a cave. It was dark. She stopped for a moment, trying to discern with her spirit. She suddenly felt repulsed. There was a strong, repugnant odour and an oppressiveness that seemed to fill the air. There were dark spirits in there.

"Where are you going, Sherry? I think we should go back. It could be dangerous."

She stopped and turned to him. "I know she's in there, Adrian. Please pray with me." She held on to his hands, and they prayed and asked for protection. She could feel Adrian's uncertainty, but she had to go in. She had no choice.

Adrian was a new Christian and only recently had been attending church with her, and where these experiences were commonplace to her, to him, it could be frightening. It was imperative that he keep his focus, guarding his mind and spirit.

They both used the torch lights on their phones and took tentative steps forward as the path became narrower and darker. The darkness of the cave was so thick that it was tangible. They could barely see as they walked deeper into the cave. The oppressive presence became stronger, so she began to sing. She held on to Adrian's hand. "Sing with me," she said, and then sang the first song that came to mind: "For Thou, oh Lord art high, above all the earth…"

Adrian joined in, their voices echoing through the cave and seeming to reverberate back towards them, making it sound like many were singing along with them. As they sang, she waited on the Holy Spirit for an answer.

Suddenly, a bright light became visible beside her, then an angel who was so much taller than they were appeared. He was dressed in armoured clothing with a sword in his hand. The light that shone from him eliminated the darkness around them. It was so bright that it made it difficult to make out his face.

She felt Adrian's hesitation, then fear, so she leaned into him and squeezed his hand in reassurance.

"Are you seeing what I'm seeing?" Adrian whispered into her ear.

They continued on. "Yes," she whispered back, and smiled. "It's amazing, isn't it? God is here."

"Yes," he said with a smile. Although she couldn't see his face, she knew that he was smiling by the change in his tone. He said it wistfully, as if astounded at the sight before them, and she could also feel the lift in his spirit.

The angel suddenly lifted his arm to stop them and pointed a few steps ahead to a dip that would have made them fall into what looked like a huge, rocky crater.

Shocked at their close call, Sherry felt her heart jolt and took in a breath. "Thank you, my Lord," she whispered, grateful for His protection. That would have been seriously bad for them both.

Then the angel pointed to a drop in the cave, and there was Cheryl, lying on the ground. She looked unconscious, sprawled out on her back, but the predicament that became very frighteningly apparent was that she wasn't alone. There were three huge, dark spirits surrounding her. They were doing something, but Sherry didn't know what.

She felt anger rise within. She would not let them take her friend. She prayed for the Holy Spirit to enter in, then took spiritual authority over the situation and declared protection over Cheryl.

Lord, how do we get down there? How do we get Cheryl out?

The angel pointed to some rocks to the side, showing them that they would have to climb down.

"Let me go first," Adrian said, positioning himself to descend backwards then slowly climbing down. When he was partway, he waited for her, helping her step in the right places where the rocks had eroded. He caught her waist and supported her as she stepped down. She wondered if he could smell the putrid odour that filled the air. It was so dark, and she was grateful for the light that emanated from the angel. She continued to pray.

The three dark spirits seemed to merge into one and became one huge spirit, then they addressed the angel: "You have no business here." Their voices were distorted, the sound of three merged into one.

They had every intention of taking Cheryl. They shifted their position as if guarding their prize. Were they going to do battle with the angel? Did they seriously think they could win? Sherry prayed in tongues, asking for God's protection over Cheryl. She pleaded Jesus' blood over the situation, and no sooner had the prayer left her mouth, the dark spirits began to whine and moan. "Noooo, leave us alone. Nooo…"

As she prayed, she felt the atmosphere transform, and more angels appeared, bringing with them God's radiant light. The more she prayed, the more God's presence took hold, and further groups of angels appeared. She didn't know what Adrian could see. But she could feel his fear again. She grabbed both his hands. "Pray, Adrian." She continued to pray with him, and as more angels entered in, the darkness diminished, and so did the dark spirit's power. They separated into three again, and their screams became loud and piercing. But she kept her focus on God, praying harder and squeezing her eyes shut. There was one more loud, harrowing scream, and then they fled.

By then the area was filled with angels. An effervescent light descended into the cave and became a sudden burst of colourful prismatic light. It was beautiful, no longer dark and ominous. Angels surrounded the cave, and she could see a blue lagoon that wasn't visible before. God's presence filled the cave. She felt peace and a wonderful joy, and she wanted so much to bask in it, but she needed to see if Cheryl was safe.

Oh, Lord Jesus, thank you for protecting us. Thank you for being here within me. I love you so much, but I ask, please let Cheryl be all right. Don't let her life be taken. She belongs to you.

She looked at Adrian, and he was looking around the cave and seemed stunned. This was an experience he would never forget. God Almighty's magnificent power manifested.

Sherry rushed to Cheryl. She hadn't moved since they arrived, and had a grey pallor. "Cheryl?" Sherry checked her pulse. Thankfully, she was still breathing. Sherry shook her. "Cheryl, please wake up."

Cheryl moaned and opened her eyes, placing a hand to her head. Sherry could see blood where she must have hit her head.

"Are you okay, Cheryl?"

She appeared delirious for a moment, then responded, trying to get up. "My head hurts, and my ankle." Cheryl squinted, adjusting her eyes to the light.

Sherry helped her up to a sitting position.

Adrian knelt beside Cheryl, but when he touched her ankle, she screamed out in pain. "It looks like it may be broken. It's badly swollen."

"I fell and hit my head…in the dark. I didn't see the drop," Cheryl said, her words slow and deliberate. No doubt she was concussed.

"Why did you come here by yourself?" Sherry asked. "I was scared, Cheryl."

Tears came to Cheryl's eyes. "I know, I'm sorry. I had an argument with Jeff. I shouldn't have gone off…" She burst into tears, and Sherry hugged her close.

"We've got to get out of here." Adrian stood. "I might have to carry you on my back."

Sherry looked up at Adrian, grateful he was with her. She wouldn't have been able to do this on her own. But then she looked around the cave again, she wasn't on her own. The cave was filled with angels that God had sent to protect her. She wasn't on her own at all.

<u>**10**</u>

Eventually, Keith whisked Cheryl away, and they took a seat amongst the guests as they waited. Soft music was being played by the band that had been set up nearby. The wedding would begin soon.

Sherry looked at her watch, wondering where Adrian was. There was still no sign of him. Maybe she was mistaken and he wasn't attending the wedding after all.

"Look." Candace nudged Sherry with her thigh and nodded, indicating to the guests on the other side. Sitting there with his wife was Jeff. Sherry had been in America when he got married. She couldn't attend the wedding, as her father was ill at the time.

His wife looked pretty. It was a shame that he and Cheryl didn't make it, but Sherry wondered if somewhere along the line they'd all made wrong decisions, and now, years later, memories and regret were all they could hold on to.

When Sherry found out her father was ill, it was a decision she'd grappled with for weeks. In the end, she had no choice but to support him. It wasn't really a consideration. It was her duty as his daughter. The thing she wrestled with the most was whether she and Adrian would make it to the other side of the predicament. After all, he was to be her husband—surely their love should have withstood the storm that hit them—but clearly their love wasn't strong enough. She had to accept that he didn't love her how *she* loved him, and it was the most painful hurt ever.

* * *

"Are you going to talk to me, or am I going to get one-syllable responses for the rest of the evening?"

She turned herself towards the window and ignored him.

"What's wrong, Sherry? You're making me nervous, and I don't like feeling like this."

He always did that. He was so expressive, telling her how he felt and how what she did had an impact upon him. They'd never argued before, so when she was annoyed at him, it was difficult to stay angry. But she had every right to be angry; he was hiding things from her, and they were supposed to be getting married. If she couldn't trust him now, what would it be like when they got married? She folded her arms. "I'm fine, Adrian."

"You're clearly not fine. Talk to me, Sherry."

She made no response, then noticed they were not going in the direction of her home. "Where are we going?"

"To my place to have a discussion about what is bothering you, like adults."

He was always so mature and reasonable. She would have preferred to just go home in a huff and not speak to him for a few days. It wouldn't resolve things, but she would feel a whole lot better wallowing in her hurt.

She said a silent prayer of forgiveness for her thoughts and turned to him. "Take me home, please?"

He pulled over and parked. "So we either discuss things at my place, or here for all to see and hear all our business."

"Why don't you just take me home?"

"Okay, so you want to discuss what's wrong when we get to your home, then? Is that what you prefer? Because I'm not going to leave this. I don't want us to end tonight on anger. If I've done something wrong, then let's talk about it."

He leaned forward to try to catch her gaze, but she kept her eyes on the windscreen. She sighed. He never pushed her to do what he wanted. He could so easily have been controlling, as had been her experience with other guys, and just taken her to his home, but he allowed her the freedom to process things sensibly. She did not want to be entertainment for people out on the street or her neighbours. There was an elderly lady that lived below her, and she was worse than Sherry's mother, constantly curtain-twitching, watching, and listening for every sound or event so she could gossip about it.

"Okay, let's go to yours," Sherry said.

When they arrived, she walked in the living room and paced—it helped her to think.

Adrian placed his keys on the coffee table, took a seat on the sofa, and watched her. He did not try to touch her or draw her into his arms, which she was thankful for, because it *would have made things worse, she would have pushed him away. He was dressed in a dark suit tonight, his mother expected high standards at her home. "Your mother told me that you intend to marry Genevieve. Is that right?"*

He frowned and leaned forward, resting his hands on his knees. From his expression, he hadn't been expecting that question. "No, that's not true. I intend on marrying you."

"You never told me that you were engaged."

"It wasn't important."

"What do you mean it wasn't important?"

"I told you about Genevieve."

"But you didn't tell me you intended to marry her!"

"I didn't think it was important. We broke up."

"According to your mother, Genevieve is the right woman for you." She folded her arms, not convinced.

He stood and walked over to her. "Look, I'm sorry. Maybe I should have told you. I just don't see her as important, because we broke up. She's not a part of my life anymore." He reached out to her.

She stepped away. "What about Isabella? You neglected to tell me about her, too."

He looked away. "She wasn't worth mentioning either."

"Or you just didn't want me to know. Am I third time lucky? Do I get the prize?"

Adrian returned his gaze to hers. "Sherry, that's not called for."

"So what do you expect me to think? Your mother said I'm just your plaything."

"That's not true!" He sighed, took her hand, and gently pulled her down to sit on the sofa. "Listen, my mother has her own agenda, and I won't go into details right now, but there is

nothing between me and Genevieve." He rubbed his thumb softly against her palm, which caused her stomach to tighten and butterflies to flutter.

"And yes, you are the third woman I've asked to marry me—not because I don't know my own mind, but because I have always said that I didn't want to date lots of women. I wanted to find my mate and spend the rest of my life with her. I met Isabella when I was seventeen. I didn't ask her officially; we just said we would at some stage. But she moved away, and it became difficult. Long-distance relationships don't work, and she ended it between us. Genevieve was a friend of the family. My father and her father were business associates, and when they had their business dinners, they brought Genevieve. We became friends, and our parents wanted us to marry— they still do. But I realised it's not what I want. I want you."

"So what is the agenda?"

He frowned, appearing reluctant to reply. "My mother wants to merge businesses with Genevieve's father, now that my father is gone. She wants to ease the burden from herself because I can't manage two businesses on my own." He met her gaze again. "A type of arranged marriage, that was part of the deal. Then I met you."

"An arranged marriage? Are we living in the Dark Ages?"

"It's more commonplace than you realise. My parents' marriage was arranged."

"And you want the same life?"

"No, I don't."

"Oh, so you don't love, Genevieve?"

"I like her. She's nice, but no, I don't love her."

Like her? What did that mean? Was he still in contact with her? Were they still friends? His tone and reference to Genevieve was one of affection. Sherry felt jealousy rise in her chest. She pulled her hand away from his grasp. "So why don't you marry her, since you like her so much and everything seems to be all planned and ready to go?"

"Because she isn't the one I want to be with. You are."

And what could she say in response to that?

Nothing.

All the anger and jealousy dissipated, and she allowed him to draw her into his arms. Then she rested her head on his chest and exhaled.

* * *

Sherry looked behind her, and a woman stepped out onto the sand, making her way towards them. It was the woman Sherry had seen in the white bikini, and then she saw the little girls, who ran ahead and found seats in a row near the front. The girls were in pink dresses, their hair neat and perfect, with bouncy curls. Genevieve looked the part of a wealthy wife of an entrepreneur. She was elegant in a cream designer dress, her long hair a torrent of curls around her face and shoulders. She was beautiful—unlike *her*. Sherry would never have been able to compete with a woman with such grace and sophistication.

Although Sherry was successful, her lifestyle comfortable and her business lucrative, she would never fit his class. She would never be middle-class elite. She was just *Sherry* and always would be. She didn't know how to be anything else. And maybe she needed to accept that Adrian's mother had been right all those years ago. She would never have fit in, and maybe this was what God was trying to show her.

But before she could think anymore about it, *Adrian arrived.*

<u>11</u>

When he opened the door, she fell into his arms. She couldn't stop crying, and he pulled her tightly against him as she sobbed long and hard right there on his doorstep. Eventually he lifted her into his arms, kicked the door shut, and carried her into the living room. He sat her on his lap and held her as she cried some more.

He gently stroked her back and murmured soft, soothing words.

Every so often, she heard the sound of his phone pinging as messages came through, and there were a few missed calls. He was busy and should have been working, but he never once left her side or took the calls. He just held her close, giving her the comfort she needed.

"I'm going to miss him," she said.

"I know. So am I."

She smiled through her tears. "He didn't like you very much. He was a jealous cat." Pebbles had wandered into her flat one day, hungry, lonely, and wet. Ever since, he'd never left. He was old and a little bedraggled, his black fur sleek in parts but patchy in others, and his blue eyes were always filled with love. He'd chosen her, and she loved him. When the vet called to say they had to put him down, she'd been distraught. He'd been poorly for a while, and there was nothing more they could do.

"Yes, I remember that time when we were watching TV and he hopped up on the sofa and positioned himself in between us, and every time I tried to hold your hand or touch you in any way, he growled. He guarded you like a father would."

She chuckled, remembering. "Yes, he did." Her smile faded as sadness filled her again. "I loved him, Adrian."

He kissed her forehead and drew her closer. "I know, babes. I know."

* * *

"It was a beautiful ceremony, wasn't it?" Candace sipped her wine. "It brought tears to my eyes."

"Yes, if you like that sort of thing," Sherry said. "I don't like weddings, remember?" They stood in the hotel reception room being served cocktails and entrees, waiting for the wedding party to arrive. The last of the family photos were being taken on the beach.

Candace rolled her eyes. "Oh yes, how could I forget. You complain every time we attend one."

Sherry nervously sipped on her fruit punch, scanning the room. *Where is he?* Her stomach was doing somersaults and she felt sick inside. From the moment she'd spotted him, her eyes had been glued on him. She'd barely taken note of the ceremony, *only him*, and it was a wonder she'd made it through without hyperventilating. Every time he turned, her heart skipped a beat as she wondered if he'd noticed her or even knew she was there. Candace hadn't helped her nerves when she'd suddenly shrieked.

"Isn't that Adrian?" Candace looked at Sherry, shocked. "He's the best man…"

By that point, Sherry was so nervous that she was gripping the chair. She was sure she must have looked pale, because Candace was staring at her.

"Are you all right?" Candace asked. "Do you want me to get you a drink?"

Sherry gave a short shake of her head, her eyes fixed on Adrian. Then she saw him look over at his daughters, and she was able to see his profile. They waved, and he smiled and waved back, but the lady with the huge yellow hat sitting in the row in front shifted, blocking Sherry's view. She shifted to her left to see him, but by then, he was facing the front again. Her heart sank. She knew it was him—her spirit told her it was, and Candace had confirmed it—but she just needed to see his face full on.

Her heart continued to race, and then the music rose and the wedding march began and everything seemed to move into slow motion when he and the groom turned to wait for the bride to proceed down the aisle. And then Sherry saw his face.

It was him. It was him…

Candace nudged her out of her thoughts.

"There are some mighty nice-looking men here tonight."

Candace was watching a group of men by the bar but eyeing one man in particular; a gorgeous, dark-skinned man, dressed sharply in a designer suit and shiny shoes. Sherry rolled her eyes.

"What? *You* might be past it, but I'm not. I intend on having some fun while you reminisce over old times and your ex, who is clearly enjoying his life and has moved on. It's about time you did too." Candace gave her a pointed look.

"I know. I guess I just need closure."

"The man is married with a family. How much more closure do you need?"

Sherry sighed and looked away. During the photo session, Adrian hadn't glanced her way once. He looked so handsome as he smiled for the camera next to the groom and the many subsequent photographs after that. Surely he must have known she was there; Marcie would have told him. But Marcie hadn't told *her*. Putting that aside, even if Marcie hadn't told him, surely he must feel her. Their spirits had connected fifteen years ago, regardless of the fact that they'd gone their separate ways. True love never totally disappeared, did it?

Well, it hadn't for her.

The wedding party arrived. The bride and groom entered first, followed by the bridesmaids and then Adrian.

She waited in anticipation of his acknowledgement, daring him to look over at her.

He sat beside the groom, then leaned over and said something to him. Beside him, the maid of honour took a seat, and it was then that he looked directly at Sherry, his eyes meeting hers, confirming that he'd known all along that she was there.

She held his gaze, and it was like the last fifteen years fell away. She felt it, the intensity of what they'd always shared. It was like a rush of emotion hit her from across the room. She took in a breath, her heart pounded hard, and butterflies fluttered in her stomach. She'd been praying for this moment for so long, and now that it was here, she didn't know what to do.

His eyes drifted, taking in her length. She felt a blush rise to her cheeks and a rush of heat sweep through her body at his slow deliberation.

He looked the same, slightly older, his hair short and neat, shorter than he used to wear it, but he was still a good-looking man, in a tailored wedding suit that fit perfectly over his broad frame. She couldn't make out the look in his eyes, and then one of the servers stood before them, blocking their view.

She expelled her breath, not realising she'd been holding it the whole time, grateful for the reprieve. Then they were led to a table along with the gathering crowd.

She was seated in the middle at a round table with four other guests and Candace placed beside her. From the angle she was sitting, her view was obscured by a couple who were the groom's family members. They exchanged pleasantries as servers approached with bottles of wine.

What was Adrian thinking? Did he hate her?

No, hate was a strong word. Hate would mean he had strong feelings for her, but that was no more. He had a lovely family now. She watched as his wife and daughters were shown to the head table.

Well, she hoped they could at least have a conversation and lay some things to rest. She truly hoped that what he felt wasn't indifference.

Later on, when Adrian announced he was MC, she was reminded of how humorous he was. Where he stood at the front, she had a clear view of him, but never once did he meet her gaze again. He had everyone laughing, giving speeches and telling stories of the couple. The whole time, she couldn't take her eyes off him, remembering moments of them together.

Candace and the guests at their table tried to engage her in conversation, but her eyes would drift again and again to Adrian, and then she would go on a journey in her mind. She wished she could forget the memories of their time together, the way he looked at her and held her. The joy she derived from just being with him and making him happy. He'd been her world. All the love she felt back then was still there. It had never diminished. And now, she found herself loving and wanting a man that was no longer hers to have.

On a sigh, she tried her best to focus on the conversation around the table, but found that difficult. She looked down at her half-eaten plate of mixed green salad with a raspberry-infused vinaigrette that was no longer appetising.

She couldn't help but find her gaze returning to Adrian as he moved to sit with his family. He was helping the younger of the two girls eat. Her heart swelled. He'd turned out to be the good father she always knew he would become. She couldn't help but imagine how he would have been towards their children, the children they'd intended to have, but just then his wife leaned over and whispered something in his ear, and they both laughed, and then the children joined in. They looked happy, Adrian especially, and Sherry was pleased for them, she truly was.

Then why did she feel like she was reliving the pain deep in her heart for a second time?

After the first course had been served, she looked around the room. Everyone looked so happy, laughing and being merry. It was far from what she was feeling right now. She looked down at her plate that had just been placed before her—herb-roasted chicken and rice with fresh apricot. She wasn't sure about the apricot and looked at it dubiously. She lifted her fork, but just couldn't bear to eat anymore. She felt so sick inside.

She decided to take a walk. Candace was in deep conversation with the man from the bar. Mark seemed quite taken with Candace, and Sherry wanted to give Candace the space she needed. Besides, she felt like the fifth wheel, and there was a lot of smiling and giggling going on.

Sherry removed her sandals and walked down to the beach. She glanced at the wedding altar and chairs and wondered at her fate. Why hadn't it happened for her? She'd contemplated it over the years. She had such a longing in her heart. A longing for *him*.

She wanted to cry.

Turning one chair to face towards the ocean, she took a seat and placed her sandals on the sand. She took in salty scent of the sea in the air as it brushed against her face. The waves rolled in and out, and the sun glowed in the sky. It was a beautiful sight.

She hated weddings.

Maybe she should just retire to her hotel room for the evening. They wouldn't miss her. She didn't want to pretend and hide how deeply she felt about the situation and the resentments she'd felt at the time. In her heart, she'd forgiven all. She'd prayed about it, and this, she hoped, would be the final step to her release from the torture of loving the man she couldn't have.

* * *

She'd been summoned.

Sherry looked down at her phone and disconnected the call from Ann, Miriam's P.A. Miriam wanted them to meet at five thirty p.m. at her home in Kensington. She wondered why, but figured that she wanted to talk to her about the wedding preparations. Right now, it was far from what she wanted to discuss. Her father was ill, having just been diagnosed with cancer, and she was worried.

Since her parents' divorce, her father had remained single, his only immediate family was her, and Angela was too young. He'd asked Sherry many times over the years to move to Atlanta, to develop her relationships with his siblings and many cousins over there. She'd promised, but never did.

Now that he was ill, she wanted to be with him, and she wasn't fully sure how Adrian felt about it, although she could take a guess; he'd been distant with her. But it would only be for a little while, until her father's treatment schedule was stable. They'd discussed it and planned to talk some more about it that evening, as she was leaving the following week.

She shut her laptop down and checked the time on the wall clock in her office. It was four fifteen. She had enough time to get there. There was a direct train, but she'd better get her skates on. Glancing down at her suit, she was thankful that she hadn't dressed down today. Hopefully she would pass Miriam's high standards.

Sherry rushed out, saying a hasty goodbye to her co-workers, then texted Adrian letting him know she would be late.

Why are you going to be late?

I'm on my way to your mother's.

Why?

She asked me to meet her.

Oh. She didn't tell me. Do you want me to come?

Yes.

Okay, I'll meet you there, but I'll be a little late, as I'm in the middle of something at the moment. I'll be with you soon. Love you.

Disappointed, she stared at the phone. She really didn't want to meet his mother on her own. She sighed and asked God to give her strength, then responded. Love you too. x

When she finally arrived after the hectic train ride, packed with commuters, she walked the length of the long drive, which took an age, and wished she'd called a taxi from the station.

The door opened as soon as Sherry approached, and Miriam greeted her with a soulless gaze. Miriam led Sherry into her office, and Sherry took the seat opposite her desk.

"I hear your father is ill. How is your family coping with the news?"

"Not very well. He will need to start chemotherapy soon."

"How are you coping?"

"I'm worried, obviously, but once I see him, I'll feel better about things." Miriam was asking all the right questions for someone who had just learned about a family member having cancer, but there was no empathy in her eyes, no love or concern. So why the questions?

"And you are travelling over next week?"

"Yes."

"Then don't come back."

Sherry looked at her in shock. Had she heard wrong?

"The timing fits perfectly. You and I know you are not the right woman for my son. We have spoken about this before. I just feel it would be best for you and Adrian not to drag this out any further." She gave a pained smile. "I know this might be upsetting, but think about this logically. How

can you run your father's company, be a support to your father while he is ill, travel back and forth from America to England, and then, in between all that, be there for my son? It just is not going to work, and I don't want you to subject my son to that kind of pain."

Sherry said nothing, not quite comprehending what Miriam was saying.

Miriam opened a drawer and pulled out an envelope. "You haven't been working for long, and with your move and everything, this will make things easier." She handed Sherry the envelope.

Sherry stared at her, still not understanding what was happening.

"Open it. See it as a gift, on the condition that you leave now, and don't ever contact my son again."

Sherry reached for it automatically then looked inside the envelope. There was a cheque inside in the amount of one hundred thousand pounds. She returned her gaze to Miriam's. Her eyes were cold like steel.

Sherry looked away, then stood on shaky legs, feeling tears sting her eyes.

"Trust me, it is better if it is done now, before things become even more difficult. Let him go, Sherry. Let him have the life he is supposed to have with a good woman by his side. The wedding plans are all in place. Genevieve is waiting for him..."

Miriam continued to talk, but Sherry was no longer listening. She turned and walked out, closing the door behind her.

* * *

Sherry prayed. There was hardly anyone on the beach. It was late afternoon, most guests were in the restaurant, and the others were at the wedding. Grateful to have some time alone, she tried to settle the restlessness she felt. There was a lone jogger making the most of the quiet and the beautiful sunset of red, orange, and gold.

Although the sight was amazing, he couldn't see the majestic sight *she'd* been graced with. Angels were lined up along the water's edge. And as she prayed, more angels appeared. They were dressed in white; the male angels were in trousers and shirts and female angels in mid-length dresses. Because of the way they were dressed, she knew it was something major that would involve many people.

She looked up, and there was an opening in the clouds and a bright light from which the angels descended.

Then she felt the uneasiness. *What's wrong, Lord? "Pray, Sherry."*

She glanced at the hotel, and there, sitting over the restaurant roof, were two dark spirits. They were misshapen figures of a dark, shadowy mist, with a strong presence of evil. She knew their names it dropped in her Spirit—*Mischief.*

A feeling of dread filled her. What mischief would they create?

Through the windows to the restaurant all the guests were having their evening meal. It was bustling and packed with people, and she suddenly felt afraid of what was about to happen.

"Do not fear. I am here. Continue to pray."

Sherry did as she was told as more and more angels descended and made their way to the hotel. The dark spirits had no choice but to flee when God's presence took hold, and then it happened: a loud boom thundered through the hotel, smashing glass in its wake.

The explosion jolted her into shock for a moment, then she heard screams and people rushing to get out. Her first thoughts were of Candace, then Adrian, Marcie, and all the wedding guests. She jumped up in haste to warn them, but the Holy Spirit shouted within, *"Do not move! Pray."*

She conceded and continued to pray, watching the chaos unfold before her.

There was smoke coming from the kitchen area. People screaming, rushing to get out, some women and children crying as the angels guided them out. But they couldn't see this, of course, and regardless of their beliefs, God still protected them.

Then Sherry saw Candace with Mark, and he was holding her close as they stepped outside. Then Adrian with his family, Marcie, Jake, and the wedding party. It would seem everyone was safe.

Sherry sighed with relief and thanked God for his mercies. She couldn't see the angels anymore, but she knew they were still there. She felt at peace that no one was hurt. God had halted the enemy's plans today.

Before long, the beach became crowded. From where she was standing, she couldn't see anyone from the wedding, but continued to pray, then heard Candace's screech. "Sherry! *Sherry!* Where are you?"

Sherry called out, as the crowd was too dense to even try to make her way over to her friend, and realised belatedly that Candace may have thought she was still in the hotel. "I'm here!" She waved a hand above the crowd. "I'm all right!"

After a moment, she saw the crowds begin to part to reveal not only Candace, but Adrian too. Sherry's throat tightened, and she was sure she felt the ground shake, because she was about to come face to face with the one and only man who had meant everything to her. Then, all of a sudden, she became aware that she couldn't breathe.

<u>12</u>

"Are you okay? I was so scared. I thought you were inside." Candace approached, stricken with worry.

Sherry's legs seemed to buckle. She took in air, gasping for breath. Candace caught her arm. "Oh my God, she must have inhaled some smoke—" Candace said to Adrian.

"No, I'm fine." Sherry took in a deep breath then slowly raised her eyes and met Adrian's intense gaze. She felt it again, and the force that hit her was more intense than before. She felt heat rush through her, and her legs began to tremble.

"Are you sure you're okay?" he asked.

She blinked for a moment. He was actually talking to her. His deep, smooth voice was exactly the same, and there was concern in his eyes. Words momentarily failed her as she stared at him. Up close he looked good, even more handsome than before. His tie and jacket were discarded, his broad muscular

110

frame filled out his shirt, the two top buttons were undone, revealing his wide neck. He was the same, but older; his youthful look had gone, replaced with a look of wisdom and maturity. He'd always been ahead of everyone else, but now there was something else in his eyes that said he'd experienced *life*. Suddenly she was so filled with joy that all she wanted to do was to fling her arms around his neck and hug him. She took a deep breath to try to calm her racing heart. "Yes, I'm fine." She gave a faint smile. "I was outside when the explosion hit. I think it happened in the kitchen."

"Oh thank God." Candace touched a hand to her chest. "I was worried."

They could barely be heard above the sirens and raised voices. Smoke was billowing from the hotel into the sky, seeming to fuel the chaos. But all she could do was stare into Adrian's eyes, and when he took a step back, for the first time, she realised he was guarding himself.

There were a few moments of pause where they stared at each other, neither knowing what to say.

"How have you been?" Adrian asked finally.

Not good. I've missed you for fifteen years. She clasped her hands together to stop herself from reaching for him. "It's been busy. It's good to see you, Adrian." She searched his gaze. His eyes became shuttered, and she felt his unease. Her heart squeezed. She wanted to touch him. "What about you? I see you have a lovely family."

"Yes. I got married." He dropped his guard for a moment and looked at her pointedly, as if to say he'd married someone else because she didn't want him. But that was so far from the truth. She'd never stopped wanting him, loving him. She'd ached for his presence and was so filled with joy at having a chance to talk to him now.

"I can see that you two need some time alone, so I'm going to join the others," Candace announced.

Sherry nodded, barely acknowledging Candace as she left. The crowd had dispersed along the shore; they walked further down, as the hotel staff were not allowing anyone in until the fire crew had finished up in the kitchen. The fire was out, but they were ensuring everything was safe before anyone could return.

She kept her eyes on him. "I know, I heard. It hurt." She knew they did not have long. His family would be calling him soon, and she wanted to say what she should have said all those years ago.

He looked at her. "Really? You didn't want me, Sherry. So why would it hurt?"

"Adrian, of course I wanted you…" She trailed off. She didn't even know how to begin to tell him how she felt, how intimidated she was by his mother and how unsure she was of his love.

He stopped walking and stared at her. "Then why did you leave? Why walk out on me when we planned to be married?"

There was anger and pain in his eyes. She hadn't expected that. She thought he would have gotten over her a long time ago.

"I'm so sorry I hurt you. It wasn't my intention to hurt you. I didn't want to leave, but I was afraid… I guess I shouldn't have been intimidated by your mother."

"What?" He looked at her, confused.

He doesn't know. She thought he knew. "Your mother—"

"Daddy!" His daughters came running up the beach towards them. They ran into his legs. "We're hungry, Daddy."

He looked down at them and hugged them close. "I know. It won't be for much longer, I promise. Aunt Suzie always has something in her handbag. Did you ask her?"

They shook their heads.

They were adorable. Sherry could see the resemblance to Adrian, but they also had their mother's features. Their eyes were lighter brown, and their complexion was lighter too. Adrian was fair-skinned due to his father being Caucasian, and the girls' complexion favoured their mother's. But their smile was the same. Adrian always had a nice smile. He must be so proud. Then she absently wondered who Aunt Suzie was.

"I want you to meet someone," he said to them. He returned his gaze to hers. "This is Sherry. She's an old friend of mine."

"Pleased to meet you. I'm Hannah, and this is Emily," the older one said.

Hannah and Emily? Sherry's mind flashed to the flight attendants; she realised that God had answered when she asked what their names were, in His own unique way. She felt her heart lift and smiled. *God always answers.* "Hello, it's nice to meet you too." She reached into her handbag. "I loved the hors d'oeuvres so much that I stashed some away for later." Sherry smiled and pulled out neatly folded serviettes. She opened them up to reveal six cheese and tomato bite-sized quiche things. She handed them to Hannah and Emily.

The girls grinned. "Thank you!" they said, and sat on the sand, sharing the snacks equally.

Adrian looked at Sherry and gave her a half-smile that didn't quite reach his eyes. "You still do that? Save snacks for later so you don't have to cook?"

She smiled. She was notorious for that, and would store them in the fridge for a midnight snack or a meal the following day. "Yes, I never did marry that special someone who loved me enough to cook for me."

He looked at her, knowing exactly what she meant, that *he* had been the one. But it was all too late now. "Do you think that—"

"Adrian!" Jake waved at the entrance to the hotel. "They're calling us back in now!"

Adrian acknowledged him as the crowds made their way back inside. "I've got to go back." He paused for a moment, seeming to want to say something, but didn't know how to. "It was good seeing you again, Sherry." He turned away. "Come on, girls, let's go back in." He ushered them up and guided them along as a father would, holding their hands, one on either side.

Was that it? Was that all he had to say to her?

She had so much she wanted to say, so much she wanted to apologise for. But he didn't seem to care…

No, that was a lie. She'd felt his hurt. There was some resentment there, too.

Is this what you wanted to show me, Lord, after all these years? That I hurt him so much that he hates me?

Her heart felt like it was breaking again, and when the tears came, she couldn't hold them back.

* * *

He looked up from his laptop. "Promise me that we'll always be close, Sherry."

She reached out and stroked his forearm. "Of course we will," she replied, wondering if he was beginning to feel what she had been feeling for a while now.

"I have a confession to make. You know how much I love what I do?"

She nodded.

"I don't want to give it up, but Mother is putting pressure on me to continue the family business. It will be impossible to do both."

"What if you employed more staff?"

"I could do that, but the ultimate decision would fall to me. There is no one who can take my place, and I have staff who rely on me."

She'd noted the change in him. It was becoming a strain trying to manage everything. She'd tried to help as much as she could in the evenings and weekends. They worked until gone eleven, and then she would go home and roll into bed until another full day. She was tired, and so was he. They did nothing but work, and they'd stopped talking.

Most evenings, she couldn't help but gaze at him. She would look over at his profile and take him in, and occasionally he'd look up from his laptop and glance at her and smile. And then sometimes he'd lean over and kiss her.

There wasn't anything wrong with their relationship, but it wasn't right. *She worried that it was beginning to fray at the edges, and she didn't know how to repair it.*

And then she found she began to preserve her heart.

Maybe it was selfish of her to not try to salvage what wasn't quite right, but she was afraid his mother's influence would be stronger than their love. With the pressure on him being the head of the family and the estate, she didn't want to influence him away from who he was supposed to be. It wasn't her choice to make, no matter how much she wanted Adrian to choose her.

The truth was, she couldn't imagine ever fitting into his lifestyle, fit in with the type of people that made up Adrian's business and family life. She didn't look the part, and maybe that had been the problem all along.

Her going away would be the test to see if he wanted a lifetime with her.

And then she had to ask herself, what right did she have to make him choose?

"So what are you going to do?"

"I don't know, Sherry. I was hoping that you would hold the reins. You *I can trust, and I know you can handle it."*

Flabbergasted, she stared at him. "But I don't have the experience, Adrian."

"I will be here to guide you." He grinned, because she was sure her face was a picture of pure astonishment. "Just think about it and then we'll talk." He kissed the tip of her nose. "All I know is, as long as you're here by my side, nothing else matters." He resumed typing again, and because she realised that his words held a deeper meaning, she stared at him for a long moment, wondering if this was his way of making her indispensable, to get his mother off his back.

"Are you okay?" he asked when she continued to stare at him.

"Yes. I miss you."

He frowned. "What do you mean? I'm right here." He reached out and caressed her cheek, then placed his hand at her neck and brought her near for a kiss. The kiss was brief, but it still made her lose all sense of control, her heart pounding to the beat of his love song and her spirit wrapped in his. But then, too soon, he returned his gaze to the laptop and resumed typing again.

⁺ ＊ ＊

When Sherry prayed, things happened. It had always been that way, from her earliest memories. God allowed her to see into the future and sometimes into the present. He allowed her to see the good and the bad, and she accepted now that they went hand and hand, but found she could influence it. She invited God in wherever she went. His presence was always with her.

Over the years, she'd prayed for Adrian, *yearned* for him. She'd always prayed that he would find happiness, but her heart had ached to see him again, and God had been merciful in granting her that. She didn't know what she expected when she met him again, what his response would be, but if she was honest with herself, she hadn't expected his dismissal of her, and it hurt deep down to her core. But then, he was married now with a family—did she expect him to declare his undying love?

No, she couldn't expect that, but nonetheless, she'd hoped they could talk. She'd felt his hurt and a touch of anger, still, after all these years. She'd wanted so much to touch him, for him to touch her as he used to. Even just a hug, to be in his arms just one more time…

Sherry couldn't bring herself to go back inside, to pretend and be merry about the coming together between a man and woman—the perfect union she would never experience in her lifetime. So she slipped to the sand and cried. Cried for what she was given and what she'd thrown away. She'd allowed the enemy to dictate to her that day, and she would forever regret not being stronger. She should have fought for who God had told her she was and taken spiritual authority. But she hadn't believed it.

She wished now that she had.

* * *

*"Jesus has given you the spiritual authority to take power—*authority *over all situations. Sickness and disease, raising the dead, and casting out demons." Pastor Chris looked up from his Bible at the pulpit. "If you don't receive God's promises, it's because you do not operate in your authority."*

"What are you focusing on? Are you focused on your problems or are you focused on God?"

They were questions that began a debate with the church youth group. Adrian had questions, and seemed to have quite a number that continued in the car on the way home.

"So you can take authority over every situation?" Adrian asked.

Sherry smiled. She loved the way he was so inquisitive. It was the way his mind worked; he had to process things through questioning. "Yes, He gives you the anointing to do that. We must not fear. We have to stand up and fight, being the warriors that we are."

She looked out the window as they crossed London Bridge and the River Thames in the distance. The sun was bright today and reflected on the water like floating crystals. High above, the twin towers loomed as they drove through. Her eyes automatically drifted upward, taking in the intricate detail of the architecture that was always amazing. It was a beautiful sight. She never tired of it.

Adrian glanced at her. "So, you're a warrior? You fight?"

Sherry's smile broadened, returning her gaze to him. "Yes, there is a battle every day in the spiritual realm. We just don't see it. We must pray, praise Him, and get in His presence every day. This is putting on our armour of God. He protects us every day from all manner of things, but we have to step into his protection first and put it on every day."

He frowned, becoming silent for a moment, then indicated to move into another lane. "What is the armour of God?"

"The belt of truth, the breastplate of righteousness, the shoes of the gospel of peace, the shield of faith, the helmet of salvation, and the sword of the spirit. This is our protection, and we must put this on every day."

"So, through prayer, praise, and worship, we can take spiritual authority over all things?"

"Yes." She watched him. He was still frowning, his full lips slightly parted as he contemplated what she'd told him. She could almost feel his brain churning over. She really wanted him to understand this, it was so important and the foundation he needed for his Christian walk.

"Sounds too easy to me."

"It is and it isn't. We fail because we take our focus off Jesus and focus on our problems. That's why Pastor Chris gave the illustration from Matthew 14, to show how Peter walked on water. He was able to do this because he kept his eyes on Jesus, but then he became distracted by the elements—the storms, the problems, the voices of others who told him he couldn't do it—and then he began to sink into the water. It is exactly the same with us. We must keep our eyes on Jesus and not allow others and the problems we face to distract us."

He leaned over and kissed her. "Thank you. I understand now. I know what I need to do."

She frowned. "What do you need to do?"

He smiled. "Don't worry. You'll see."

* * *

"Why are you out here on your own?" Candace asked as she approached. "Aren't you hungry? You hardly ate anything at dinner."

Sherry looked up at Candace and shook her head, brushing away her tears.

"I thought you were coming back in?" Candace looked concerned. "You've been crying. What happened? What did he say to you?" She sat on the sand beside Sherry.

"That's just the problem. He didn't say much at all. I know he's married now, but I just needed to talk to him, you know?" She rummaged in her handbag for a tissue.

"Did you tell him about his mother?"

"No, he didn't give me a chance to."

"If he couldn't spare the time to talk to you, then he's not worth even thinking about, Sherry."

That's easier said than done. "I guess. It was a bit of a shock, that's all."

"It's time to move on, Sherry."

It *was* time that she moved on, but right now, she felt sick. "I know. You're right." Sherry stood.

Candace stood too, brushing the sand off her dress.

"I'm going to go back to the hotel room."

"Why? Don't let him chase you away. We have lovely views on this beach. Let's stay out here for a while and sing to our Lord. It will make you feel better, you know it will. And then we can go back in and dance it out. Please don't let this situation get you down like it did before."

"But you can't stay out here with me. You have the wedding to attend—besides, Mark seems really interested in you."

"Mark is nice, but you come first. I'm not going to have you upset, Sherry. I'll even hike that mountain with you tomorrow."

Sherry looked at her with astonishment, then burst out laughing. "Really? You, hike that mountain? I don't think so somehow."

Candace laughed. "I would do anything for you. You're always there for me."

Sherry grinned. "Okay, Candace," she said, knowing Candace had no intention of hiking the mountain with her. "Let's sing unto our Lord."

And they did, and Sherry felt so much better.

<u>13</u>

They'd stayed in that night, at his place. Adrian had cooked pasta and she was full. "Ahh, man, I'm going to miss your cooking while I'm away." She rubbed her tummy and leaned back in the chair.

A sadness came to his eyes. He took her hand across the table. "You could stay. That way you wouldn't have to miss my cooking, and when we're married, I'll cook for you."

She grinned at that. "Sounds good to me. I'll do the washing up. I think we would make the perfect partnership." But even as she said the words, she knew it wasn't true, and she hoped on a prayer that he would love her enough to change the outcome that she'd tried so hard to fight against.

"But I have to go, Adrian. My father is seriously ill. It hurt that he hid it from me, and all this time he did nothing. I have to go." She squeezed his hand, because the hurt in his eyes seized her heart and she didn't know what else to do. "Come with me?"

"I can't, Sherry. I can't trust Gary enough to leave everything in his hands. You know the problem with him. His

gambling addiction is still causing problems. He's seeking help, but it means everything falls to me. I have staff that rely on me. And then my mother needs my help with my father's company, and it's becoming a burden. I need you, Sherry."

"I need you too, Adrian." She got up and sat on his lap, savouring the feel of his hands wrapped around her and his scent as she tucked her face into his neck. "What are we going to do?"

He said nothing in response, and she took pleasure in the way he slowly caressed her back, comforting her and easing the apprehension she felt.

She didn't want to leave him.

Sherry lifted her head and looked at him. "Could you come after, do you think? When things are a little more settled?"

"I don't know, Sherry. You're making it sound as if you're never coming back."

She saw the beginnings of tears in his eyes, and her heart wrenched with pain. She gently caressed his cheek. "Of course I'll come back. It's just that it won't be for a while. Dad has to have months of chemo, and then there's his company that I have to head, and I haven't got a clue."

"I'll help you."

"I know, but I can't say when I'll be back, Adrian."

Tears welled in his eyes. "Isabella said she would come back, and she never did."

Oh my Lord, is this the reason he doesn't want me to go?

The last few weeks he'd been moody and unsettled when she found out she had to visit her father. They hadn't argued, but he'd been quiet and distant, and she didn't know what to say to him. She had her own concerns about the situation with Genevieve. His mother wanted them to be married to save his father's company. She'd been pressuring him. The financial implications were great, and his mother wanted her agenda fulfilled, which was to merge companies with Genevieve's father. That ultimately meant marriage between Genevieve and Adrian.

She didn't want to leave him, but knew that when she did, Adrian would not be strong enough to fight against his mother's influence. That alone hurt most of all, because it said their love wasn't strong enough to sustain that. Sherry had mistakenly thought that it was.

"We'll work through it, Adrian. I promise. Please don't cry," she said as his tears rolled down his cheeks. She kissed them away, then she found his mouth and gave him a sweet but tender kiss to show him how very much she loved him. But for her it was bittersweet, and she hoped their love would withstand the circumstances that presented themselves.

* * *

Candace tried to convince Sherry to return to the wedding celebrations, but she decided against it and made her way to the hotel room. She couldn't face an evening acting as if everything was perfectly fine, when deep inside she was falling apart. She just wanted to get into bed and sleep to block out every painful thought and emotion that overwhelmed her sense of peace.

She toed off her sandals and unzipped her dress, thinking about how good Adrian looked. He hadn't really aged. It had taken all her will not to just throw her arms around his neck and hug him.

Was it wrong of her to feel that way?

He was married, after all. She didn't know how to stop how she felt.

He looked good, Lord. I miss him so.

She sighed when she received no response, took a quick shower, and climbed into bed recalling the night she'd left, just before she fell into a deep sleep.

* * *

"I don't want you to go." His eyes looked bleak.

"I have to, Adrian. My father's ill. I have no choice." She felt pain sear her heart at the expression on his face. She wanted to stay. More than anything she wanted to stay with him, but how could she? Her father needed her, and she wasn't one hundred percent sure of Adrian's love. He'd changed into faded jeans, and a shirt that fit perfectly across his broad chest and arms, accentuating his strong muscular definition. He was so handsome and she loved to look at him.

"I know this sounds selfish, but I need you, Sherry."

"Do you, Adrian? Or do you have Genevieve waiting in the wings?"

"What made you say a thing like that?"

"Your mother seems to think so."

"This isn't about my mother. This is about us."

Sherry was miserable. Her heart was breaking. "Come with me, then. You say you love me, then come with me."

"How can I? I have a business to run! What's happening here? Are you ending things between us?"

"I just don't know if I can be who you want me to be. I love you, but you're from a different social class. Your life is so different to mine. I just don't know if we will make it, Adrian."

He pulled her towards him. "Where is this coming from? This was never an issue before. Do you really think I care about all that? I love you and want to be with you. You promised to be my wife, and I will hold you to that."

She looked into his eyes and saw the love there, but she knew deep down that it wouldn't be so. Once she left, they would part. She could already feel the pain looming in her chest.

Silence descended upon them like a heavy blanket, where neither spoke for a long moment. He ran his hands along her arms. "When are you coming back?"

She avoided his eyes. She could see the desperation there. "I'm not sure. A few months. I don't know how long my father's treatment will be." She stepped away. Her resolve was slipping, but he pulled her back. "I've got to go, Adrian. I have an early flight in the morning and I still haven't packed yet."

He hugged her tightly against him. "Please don't go, Sherry. I'm begging you."

She felt tears sting her eyes. "Why are you doing this? You know I have to go."

"I'll pay for your father's treatment, Sherry. I'll ensure he has twenty-four-hour care."

She eased back to look at him. There were tears in his eyes; it was as if he knew this would be the last time. "I would never ask you to do that, and I want to be with my father. I'm all he has. I'm sorry." She touched his face. "I love you,

Adrian." She kissed him and looked at him one last time. He looked…devastated. "I'll call you when I arrive tomorrow."

He let her go, and she never saw him again.

<u>14</u>

Sherry crept out of the door, leaving a note for Candace, who was sleeping in her room. She hit the gym for an hour, and when she headed back, Candace was still sleeping. Sherry shook her head and smiled, Candace had stumbled in at three a.m. that morning, tripping over the coffee table in the darkness, waking Sherry up.

Candace had knocked and popped her head around the bedroom door. *'I'm sorry I woke you,'* she whispered.

'No, you're not, you just wanted to gloat about what a good time you've had.' Sherry smiled and rolled over in bed to face Candace. *'How was it then? Or should I say, how was Mark?'*

'He's so nice. I think I'm in love.'

Sherry couldn't see Candace's expression in the darkness, but her tone had become wistful. Clearly she *really* liked this guy.

'We danced the night away and we lost track of time.'

'Oh you had a really *good time then,'* Sherry grinned.

'Yes, we did. He's going to call me in the morning, so I had better get some beauty sleep.'

'So you're cancelling on me, then? Where's the loyalty?' Sherry teased.

'What do you mean?' Candace asked, sounding puzzled.

"Our hiking trip."

Candace laughed. *'Night, Sherry.'* She closed the door.

Sherry giggled, as she could still hear Candace chuckling as she headed to her room.

There was no doubt that Candace was tired, but Sherry hoped she had a good time with Mark today. She wanted Candace to find some happiness. It had been a long time for her.

Sherry looked at her watch, then hurriedly made her lunch and headed out again to meet the tour bus to take her to the Blue Mountains.

Grateful there were minimal numbers on the trip, she sat right at the back, away from everyone else. When the bus driver stopped off at a hotel on the way and picked up other guests, she closed her eyes, turned to the window, and blocked everything out until she felt a sense of awareness hit her.

Continuing to keep her eyes closed, she tried to focus, but the atmosphere had changed. Her spirit was stirred. She felt the pull.

Reluctantly, she opened her eyes. There was someone here…

She sat up and looked ahead, and saw Adrian sitting at a window seat at the front. Her heart leapt and began to pound. *He's here?* Was God giving her a second chance at closure?

Watching Adrian for a moment, she took him in. He was on his own, and from where she was sitting, she could see he was wearing white shorts and a blue t-shirt—his favourite colour. She glanced down at herself. Coincidentally, she was wearing a blue vest top too. Maybe it wasn't so much of a coincidence. Maybe she was still in tune with him. She glanced down at her engagement ring regretfully. It was a reminder of what she'd once had, but was no more.

Sherry listened, discerning with her spirit, for some message or sign from God, but there was silence. *Holy Spirit?* she asked.

Then, suddenly, she was transported back to her dream. She'd remembered snippets of it that morning, but further clarity appeared as she settled back in her seat and got lost in it.

"I can't believe I'm actually doing this. You know how I am when it comes to cooking. Something's bound to go wrong." They were spending the day together at home. The girls were watching television; Sherry could see them through the open-plan kitchen.

He smiled. "Spaghetti bolognaise is easy. We'll take it slow."

Sherry smiled up at him and put on a pot of water to boil. "So oil and salt in the water? Any other secret mystery item I should add? Because it always goes wrong with the pasta."

He slipped his arms around her waist and kissed her neck. "No secret other than my love."

Turning in his arms, she wrapped her arms around his neck. "If you're going to distract me with affection, then it will definitely go wrong." She smiled and kissed him.

"I'm giving you encouragement," he said.

Grinning she said; "I need all the encouragement I can get when I'm cooking. You had better pray for me!"

His eyes grew serious and intense. "I always pray for you. I never stopped…"

She'd wondered about the dream. What did it mean? And why did she keep dreaming about them being married? Was God showing her that he prayed for her just as she prayed for him? She had so many questions and so few answers.

Did he know she was on the bus?

Sherry sighed and turned to the window again.

What did it matter, anyway? He'd moved on, and so should she.

When they arrived, she held back and allowed Adrian to walk on ahead with the group when it became apparent that he didn't know she was there. He'd made it clear that he didn't want to talk, so she would keep her distance. It was probably for the best.

She stood with the group in line at reception as they were being shown to their rooms for the night. He was at the front. A porter took his bag, and Adrian was shown to his room.

When she was eventually shown to hers, she sighed, grateful to be back again. She connected with

God here, more so than anywhere else. She dumped her bag and stepped out onto the balcony to take in the views. As always, it was spectacular.

It was early evening. The tour guide wanted them to meet at dinner to go through the plan for the following day, but she wanted to stay in her room and pray.

She sat and took in the views of the mountains and the beautiful green landscapes ahead. Then it was as if she could feel someone watching her. She felt the hairs on her arms stand on end as an awareness filled her. She looked to the right, and there, two rooms away on the balcony, was Adrian staring at her, looking surprised.

Her heart jolted and she took in a breath. She was cautious after what had happened the day before, but found herself smiling nonetheless, and then she gave a tentative wave.

"I didn't know you were here," he called out. He went to say something else, but she could see he was conscious of the couples watching them in their own balconies. He motioned to his mobile.

Ducking inside, she retrieved hers from her rucksack. She'd kept the same number over the years. She'd always hoped he would call, but he never did.

She looked at the face, and he was ringing. He was ringing!

"Hi," she answered. She stepped back out and stared at him.

"Hey." He paused for a moment as if uncertain. "Will you have dinner with me?"

She grinned, not bothering to hide the pleasure at the thought of spending the evening with him. "Yes," she said simply and she saw him smile too.

"I'll meet you in twenty minutes. I need to take a shower."

"Okay, I'll do the same."

They disconnected, and she waved again just before stepping inside. She threw the phone on the bed, hurriedly removed her top, and prayed that they would somehow be friends again, if that was possible.

* * *

Sherry's first impressions of Atlanta were of surprise and a welcoming relief that it reminded her so much of London. The hustle and bustle, the vibrancy, the feeling of success—a cultural hub that was unique, a utopia of sorts. It made her want to explore the city and get to know the people, but her focus was on her father, and she couldn't think of anything but her need for him to get well.

She stepped up her prayer, not only because she was worried that he wouldn't pull through, but also because of the great burden of managing a major company that she knew very little about.

His right-hand man—so to speak—was old-fashioned and set in his ways. Percy Chambers liked to do things his way and his way alone, and was not interested in taking orders from a woman a quarter of his age—and he had the audacity to tell her so to her face.

Sherry had to take it on her chin. She understood his type, and gained as much knowledge from him as she could, even when he tried to hide things from her, wanting to push her into a position to fail. But he didn't understand that she had God Almighty on her side. There was no way she could fail. When she put on the whole armour of God, she was unstoppable. Percy's wasted attempts were futile.

She felt the presence that followed Percy everywhere he went, and when she prayed, it caused him confusion, dissension, and anger that manifested itself one day in the boardroom.

Her father was an entrepreneur of sorts and had his hands in several pots that were owned by the company. Property, land, cars, major shares in corporations, investments—he even owned a chain of exclusive restaurants. All department heads met every Monday morning to discuss performance, marketing, and profits. Percy chaired most meetings at the beginning. She wanted to get a feel for the company, its people, who they were and what made them tick. It gave her something to do when she was alone and still so sick inside from losing Adrian—and now, potentially, she could lose her father too.

For the first time in her life, she felt low, and her only saving grace was God. He was there every step of the way. Every evening she devoured the company books, thankful for her business degree and financial experience through working at her firm in London, plus the knowledge she'd gleaned from Adrian. She would often ask herself, What would Adrian do in this situation? *Sometimes she sought advice from her father when she sat with him in the evenings just before he went to sleep, or most often she would ask God. It was terrifying and exhilarating at the same time.*

What Percy had failed to bank on was her love of talking to individuals and getting to know them on a personal level, and the insight God showed her about many in the company, from the cleaners, to those in the highest positions. She knew about their families, their passions, what was important to them, and through the many conversations, she'd found out what worked, what didn't, sought innovation, involved them in her decision making, and then rewarded them publicly for their ideas. She quickly knew whom to trust, and those she didn't grew to trust her. She knew those that worked hard and would often arrive late after seeing to her father and there would be staff working. She was amazed at their dedication, so she wanted to give them the recognition they deserved.

Percy didn't see it that way and saw staff as a commodity that should be used and thrown away if they did not conform or deliver.

Seated at the head of the large, shiny mahogany conference table, Percy took centre stage dressed in a tailored suit. He leaned back in his chair, stroking his white beard as he fired questions at nervous staff, who delivered presentations of profit margins and failures. He took pleasure in making them feel small even with a slight dip in performance. They were never good enough.

Sherry observed and listened before finally she couldn't take it anymore and interjected on his cruelty, because that was what it was. She could see the dark spirit that stood beside him, which morphed into different forms dependent upon Percy's mood and how malicious he choose to be.

Percy impatiently shoved his glasses higher on his nose. "Linda, we've been over this. Your profits are down. What are you doing to push sales up? You come with the same charts and figures, and nothing has changed. I don't want to see this again, otherwise I will have to seriously look into whether you can handle the position you are in."

There was a hush around the room, eyes looking away and down. Many in the room felt sorry for Linda but were afraid for their own jobs and what they might say about their own less than profitable targets.

Sherry stood and walked over to the chart on the board that spanned the only wall in the spacious room. The rest were walls of glass overlooking the landscape of central Atlanta. She could feel everyone's eyes upon her as she walked the length of the room. "Linda, tell me about these five areas that are making profits consistently for the last eight months." She pointed to the chart. "What are you doing here that you think could be changed in the other areas?"

Linda's eyes lit up. "It's the menu. The population in those areas are totally different culturally than the other areas. They are the affluent areas, whereas the areas falling behind are mainly our poorer areas. We need to cater to their needs, understanding the diversity of the community. Percy, I sent you a recommendation of the changes I wanted to make, but you said you wanted everything to be consistent across the entire restaurant chain—"

"Yes, that's right," Percy interrupted, leaning forward in his chair. "We are known for our exceptional cuisine, not for low-level peasant food that will bring down the standards of our name."

"Our standards do not need to be compromised if it's done in the right way," Sherry said. "There is a change needed here. Linda, I want you to send your recommendations to me. I am sure that your ideas will make the difference we need."

Percy shot out of his chair, his grey hair flopping over his forehead. "No! I've seen her recommendations, and they are weak and go against the ethos of this company, so no changes will be made. If Linda cannot make the necessary profits then she will need to find herself another job!"

Sherry kept calm, although she was irritated by Percy's arrogance, contempt, and, now, outright racism. "No, Percy. I have made a decision in this regard and the changes will be as I see fit." She held his gaze, daring him to fight her on this.

"Who do you think you are, coming in here wanting to change things? I have been running this company for more years than you have been alive! I've seen what you have been doing, and you have no say in anything that happens in this company. You are a child, and a woman, no less! So I suggest you take a seat and allow me to continue with my meeting, or leave if you cannot hack it."

She saw the dark spirit beside him expand, then shift, feeding off his anger. The words seemed to fly across the room, then hit her shield of protection and fall to the floor at her feet.

Saying a silent prayer, she drew on God's strength, then stepped closer to Percy, and as she did, the presence moved, then shrank. She stepped closer still. She would not allow this man and his resentments to rip apart her father's company, wound her staff spiritually by his words and outright disdain that was totally unwarranted. "Percy, it is you *who should leave. And I would like you to do that now. I will continue the meeting today."*

He stared at her in shock. "This is my—"

"No, this is my *company now. I have the ultimate say in all aspects of this business and going forward you need to think seriously if you want to continue on here or maybe* you *need to find another job elsewhere."*

There were a few sniggers and shocked gasps at that. Percy's eyes were filled with rage, his jaw hard, a snare at his mouth. He was so angry that he rested his hand on the table to stop it from shaking. Then she saw the dark spirit whisper something to him. "I will leave, but I will speak to your father about this. And those of you that think your jobs are secure, understand that when I am back, I will *be carrying out a review!"*

He stalked out of the room, slamming the door shut with a resounding bang. Then the room erupted with cheers, claps, and laughter. Sherry was surprised at first, then burst into laughter with them. It had been a victorious day, and one that changed her and made her a mighty warrior in the spiritual realm. It taught her that with God she was powerful. Nothing could harm her, no matter how overwhelming. He was on her side, always.

<u>15</u>

He was waiting in reception for her, looking at his phone by the time she arrived. He looked up, his eyes drifting over her, slowly taking her in. Something familiar entered his eyes, and then they became shuttered.

She'd changed into a simple cotton floral dress because it was so hot and the fabric was light against her skin, it flattered her curves. Maybe *that* was the reason for his look. But soon after, he seemed hesitant, and she saw the thought process in his eyes. She suspected he was thinking about what he would say to her.

He walked over to her. "Sherry. I wasn't expecting to see you."

"I hadn't expected to see you either." The urge to fling her arms around his neck and just hold him tight was overwhelming.

How do I turn this off, Lord?

They stared at each other for a moment. Although she'd thought about this moment for years; wished for it, and prayed, she wasn't prepared for what was about to happen between them. Her heart was pounding so hard, and her breath caught in her throat at his nearness. And she could smell his clean fresh scent from his shower and a subtle hint of his aftershave. It made her want to take a step closer into his arms as she used to.

From his expression he seemed just as taken with her, but he held back and seemed to guard himself. Something crossed his features, his jaw tightened as if a part of him was a reluctant party to this, but knowing it was fate that brought them together again and he wanted to see where it would lead. Then, he guided her into the restaurant, which was already half-full. They took seats opposite each other at the nearest table. "You didn't come back to the wedding last night," he said.

"No."

He looked at her. "Why?"

She wanted to say that she'd felt like her heart was breaking again. That she'd felt so embarrassed because she'd got it so wrong with him. That she regretted all the years away from him. That she missed him so much, and simply couldn't bear to see him with his wife and family. But she didn't say any of those things. "After speaking to you, I just...couldn't." She looked away and glanced around the restaurant that was beginning to fill up. Wooden tables and chairs with crisp white tablecloths were dotted around the room, alongside an open veranda with great views of Jamaica and the Blue Mountains in the distance.

He chose not to push her and she was grateful for his next question. "I'm surprised you remember this hike."

She looked at him again and gave a wry smile. "I hike this mountain every year since that day we visited all those years ago."

He looked surprised. "It's been fifteen years."

"Yes, it's been a long time."

A waitress appeared at their table. "Can I get you some drinks?"

They quickly looked at the menus.

"I'll have some water, please," Sherry said, surreptitiously watching Adrian as he looked at his menu. He'd changed into a loose fitting trousers and a white short-sleeved shirt. They were linen and fit perfectly on his frame. His broad chest and muscular arms were appealing. She curled her fingers into a fist, wanting to touch him as she used to. She remembered the times when they would be working, and she sat close and ran a hand along his sinewy forearm. She loved to feel the smoothness of his skin, the raised ridges of his veins, and the hardness of his muscles. He would often say, *You're distracting me, Sherry."* And she would gaze into his eyes and watch his grow intense, and then he would kiss her.

"I'll have fruit punch, please," he said now.

"Are you ready to order?" The waitress looked at Adrian.

He looked at Sherry. "What would you like?"

You. Oh gosh, were did *that* come from? She looked down at her menu again, hoping her eyes wouldn't betray her. *Sherry, he's married, stop it.* "Could I have the Escovitch fish, please?"

"I'll have the same," he said. "I can't have you choking on the bones on your own."

She laughed. When they'd hiked the mountains together all those years ago, they'd had dinner together in a lodge similar to this one, and Adrian had sat beside her, patting her back to help her release the fishbone stuck in her throat.

"I can't believe you remembered that! It was so embarrassing. Everyone was watching me as I choked my guts up! I have since mastered the skill of eating fried snapper without choking on the bones."

The waitress chuckled. "Don't worry, ma'am, we debone the fish before we serve it." With that, she left to serve another table.

He stared at Sherry for a moment, his eyes drifting over her. "You're looking good, Sherry. I never expected..." He trailed off and stared at her.

She laughed. "Did you expect me to look old and haggard?"

"No." He frowned, his expression serious, as if it was important that she understood what he meant. "You were always beautiful, Sherry. What I was going to say was that I didn't expect you to look the same. You haven't aged."

To counter the embarrassment and the blush that rose to her cheeks, she said, "You haven't aged either." *And you're even more handsome than before.* She didn't think it was appropriate to say the last part, and reminded herself yet again that he was a married man now.

There was a long moment of silence as they continued to stare at each other, and she felt a deep longing in her chest. She lowered her gaze and looked at the menu again, then said a silent prayer.

"You come here every year, did you say?" Adrian finally asked.

"Yes."

"When?"

She looked at him, puzzled by his question. "What do you mean?"

"What time of the year?"

"Usually in the latter part of the year, from September onwards."

The waitress returned with their drinks and placed napkins and cutlery on the table.

Sherry reached for her water and scanned the busy restaurant, because it was easier than having to look at him, talk to him, and act as though they were strangers. They used to be so close, and she'd missed him *so much.* She was finding this, right here, to be more than difficult.

There were mainly couples seated around the room, some singles. Any families had older children; the trek up the mountains was an intense four-hour hike and was quite difficult for an amateur. Sherry suspected that was the reason Adrian had left his family behind.

"That's why we've missed each other. I usually come here in the summer months."

Sherry looked at him. "So you visit every year too?"

"Yes."

Oh, how did I miss him? Disappointment filled her. "I always hoped I would see you."

"We come in the summer months because the girls are off school then."

"Ahh, okay, I didn't think." But then she considered that maybe they were just not supposed to meet before. So near, but yet so far.

He eyed her contemplating her response. "What were you hoping would happen if we did meet?"

She searched his eyes. "Maybe for us to talk."

"Well, we have the rest of this evening and the whole of tomorrow and our bus ride back, so we had better make the most of it."

* * *

Her heart ached. It felt like a physical pain that seized her chest and wouldn't release. She fell to the sofa and stared at the article in the local news. His family were prominent enough in the community that his wedding had hit the press: Adrian Chase, entrepreneur, married to Genevieve Shapney, the perfect union; may they have many years of wedded bliss…

Sherry's phone fell from her fingers and tears stung her eyes. So he'd married her after all, just as his mother had said.

She prayed then, prayed for healing, prayed for compassion, and, most of all, prayed for Adrian. That he would be happy and that his new bride would give him the joy and fulfilment Sherry had always wanted to bring to him.

146

<u>16</u>

She was up at three a.m., having retired early the night before, as they were leaving for the hike at five. She always slept soundly when she was here, maybe because of the atmosphere of the quiet countryside and the mountainous air, the open green foliage and the sounds of birds outside her window. Or perhaps it was the spiritual feel. God's presence was here. She took the opportunity to pray, and delighted in time spent with the Holy Spirit.

Sherry had made sandwiches for lunch; there was no time for breakfast, so she would eat on the way up. She was not only excited, but also nervous. This being the last time she would have to spend with Adrian, and she wanted to savour each moment.

Sherry made her way out. The group were gathering in the car park. Adrian was already there, messaging on his phone.

When he looked up, she expected a smile, but what she got was a hard look, his jaw rigid, his face stony.

They'd left for their rooms last night on pleasant terms, so she couldn't understand why she was on the receiving end of *that* look.

They'd kept their conversation around work. He'd asked her about her father's business, which was now half hers, and she told him of all the trials she'd had to endure and how she'd overcome. She told him about the difficulties she encountered from staff after Percy left, when she wanted to make changes to improve things. There were those that were either in Percy's camp or just did not trust a newcomer. It was *"Mr Palmer wouldn't want that changed"* or *"Mr Palmer likes things this way or that."* It got on her last nerve. The business wasn't failing, but some changes were needed in order to get ahead of the current climate, and some staff did not have the foresight to see beyond the now. Regrettably, she'd had to give some ultimatums, which had been challenging at the age of twenty-four.

She had to grow up pretty quick, and prayed *a lot*, but thankfully, although there had been conflict, she didn't have to dismiss anyone, and the business was thriving, making more profits than it had before.

Adrian told her he was proud of her, and in that moment, she realised for the first time that she'd needed his affirmation. Many of the decisions she'd made were with him in mind. It felt good to have his praise. She, in turn, asked him about his business. It was safer than asking him about his family. She just wasn't ready for a conversation about that.

"Even though our businesses merged, I still got dragged into working solely for my father's firm. The scale went into the millions. I couldn't turn my back on it. Gary heads up my business now. He's cleaned up and married with three kids."

Marriage. The dreaded word. She needed to keep well away from *that* topic. It made her think of what her life would have been like if she'd married Adrian. He'd wanted *her* to take over his business, it had seemed overwhelming when he'd made the proposal, but looking at things now and what she'd achieved with her father's company, she would have excelled at it. Adrian had been right and had faith in her, even back then. "So, you're the rich, high-flying businessman now. I always knew you could accomplish anything you wanted. You were always so driven. That was one of the things that attracted me to you. You were nearly there with your business alone, but understood you didn't want it be just handed to you, like me."

"After all the changes you made, I don't see that as being just handed to you, Sherry. You brought that business into the future, making more profits than ever before. You made that business yours."

It was true, she had. She grinned, and he smiled with her. There was a light in his eyes that made her heart flutter. But then they ran out of things to say, and he stared at her, and she stared at him.

Neither said anything for a few moments, and then he caught her hand. "I'm surprised you still wear this." He touched a finger to her engagement ring, waiting for a response, but it was evident that he felt the pull when they touched, as he quickly released her hand again.

She'd totally forgotten to remove her ring before she met him, and during the meal she'd tried to keep it hidden by keeping her hand under the table. Unfortunately, she wasn't able to eat with one hand and hadn't done a good job in keeping it hidden. She'd hoped he wouldn't notice, but clearly he had. "I've never taken it off since the day you gave it to me."

Something crossed his face as he considered her response. "Has there never been anyone? Didn't you get married or decide to?"

"No," she said, keeping her answer short. She did not want to talk about her failed love life, because it meant talking about how she still felt about him, and this was neither the time nor the place.

Silence ensued again, and she had no choice but to ask him the question that she wasn't ready to ask yet. "So, how is married life?"

Sherry saw his eyes change. They became cloudy and closed, but before she could say anything else to ease the tension and the silence that followed, the tour guide gathered everyone to meet to go through the plans for their trip in the morning, which did not leave them time to talk again afterwards. Then

Sherry had taken the opportunity to disappear to her room after saying goodnight.

Now, as she searched his eyes, she didn't know what she'd done wrong. Maybe talking to her had brought back the past and the emotional turmoil that came with it. Perhaps, after all these years, he'd suppressed his feelings and needed closure as well.

Sherry walked over to him as the group headed forward and entered the Blue Mountain trail entrance. "Morning, Adrian. Did you sleep well?"

"Not really. I had a few things on my mind."

She knew all about that. "Well, I'm sorry to hear that. Maybe the hike will clear your mind some."

"Maybe," he said, then reached for her rucksack.

"You don't have to do that. It's a long hike."

"Sherry." He raised a brow and held out his hand to take it from her. She reluctantly handed it to him, reminded of how considerate and gentlemanly he was, and for a second time, they touched. Their fingers brushed. She took in a breath at the tingle of sensation that rushed up her arm, and she fought to keep her body from trembling at his nearness. She did not have the safety of the table separating them as she had the night before when he looked at her, silently assessing her. She expected him to step away, but he didn't, and what she saw in his eyes, she couldn't quite decipher.

As the group continued on the trail, they followed at a slower pace. The trail was intense in parts, densely forested and narrow, and it was still dark, although not completely, as dawn was beginning to break.

Sherry listened for a moment to what God might want her to know and kept being reminded of her dreams. She understood now that the purpose of the dreams was to show her that she would meet him again, but she couldn't quite understand the rest and why they were depicted as being married. Perhaps it was because a piece of Adrian was still entwined in her heart.

"So how was the wedding? It must have been good. Candace got back at three."

"Yes, it was." He smiled, and it softened his face a little. "Jake and Marcie have been together for a while. It was about time that they tied the knot. They've been talking about it for years."

"I didn't know that you were close to Jake."

"We became closer in recent years. They have children the same ages as my two, so we have that in common as well."

Yes, it was something Sherry never had in common with her friends. It seemed to be the get-in-free card with most family units, having children the same age. Which meant she was always the outsider looking in. She didn't have charming anecdotes about the latest thing her son or daughter had done.

As they continued the long trek up to the peak, she barely listened to the tour guide, as she'd heard it so many times before. When they got to Yallah River, Adrian helped her across the shallow stream by taking her hand, and when he did, she was filled with a sudden, intense pain. She felt his hurt, a raw, searing ache that wrapped itself around her heart and constricted.

What is this? Why is there so much pain? She struggled for breath for a moment and stopped in her tracks after she stepped across to the other side of the river. He caught both of her arms as she stumbled.

"Are you okay?" he asked, concerned.

"Yes, sorry. I must have tripped on something." She looked at the ground so she didn't have to look in his eyes, because in that moment, she wanted to cry.

What happened to him, Lord?

"He needs your healing. Pray for him, Sherry."

Guilt pierced her soul. Was she partly to blame for the emotional turmoil he was going through?

Even though she couldn't identify any specifics, she knew instantly that some of his pain wasn't because of her. There was *something*…but it wasn't revealed to her. So she prayed for him, as the Holy Spirit asked, trying to stay focused on Him and Adrian at the same time.

The way was narrow and steep, and they barely spoke the rest of the way, other than to make the odd passing comments about the botanical flowers or to tease each other a little, the way they used to.

Adrian kept close over each and every hurdle, helping her along the way. The morning light began to break through the shadows, revealing breath-taking views over the mountain and island below.

Sherry took in the colourful wildflowers, tree ferns, and the birdsong that seemed to serenade them as they climbed higher up the mountain, breaking through the shrouded mist.

When they finally reached the peak, they stopped for lunch and admired the wonderful views. It was warm now after that long hike, and she removed her outer garments, stripping to her vest top. They sat amongst the foliage with the best views, set apart from the others in the group and stared out at the landscape in silence for a moment. They could see the ocean in the distance. The mountain was surrounded by billowy clouds. It was amazing, a majestic sight.

She suspected he wasn't just arrested by the beauty before them, but wondering how to start the conversation that must have been on his mind all the way up the trail. It had been on her mind too, yet she'd allowed the easy banter to continue, remembering fun times between them and the man that Adrian was. The way his deep baritone voice whispered along her skin. His throaty laugh that made her giggle and his wonderful smile that always warmed her heart.

Sherry rummaged in her rucksack and pulled out her lunch, then looked at him because she could feel him watching her. He had his lunch neatly packed in a plastic container, unlike hers, which was wrapped in foil and all misshapen now, as it had slipped to the bottom of her bag.

"Do you intend to share?" he asked, lifting his eyebrows.

She smiled. "You wouldn't want one of mine, but yours looks pretty good. What have you got?"

"A chicken wrap and a tuna and cucumber sandwich." He held out the container to her.

Sherry took half the wrap. "Thank you," she said, then took a bite.

"So?" he said, indicating to her lunch.

She grinned. "You won't like them. They're tomato ketchup sandwiches…"

He looked at her aghast, and she couldn't help but laugh.

He shook his head. "I see you haven't changed in that regard." He smiled a little. "Do you still eat peanut butter and pickle sandwiches? Because that is just *gross*."

She giggled. "Yes, it's my favourite. It was my dad that introduced me to those sandwiches."

"How is your father now?" he asked.

"It was difficult for a while." *Difficult* wasn't really an effective enough word to describe what she'd been through with her father. She had to reach deep within herself to withstand the spiritual elements working against them. The pain and fear had overwhelmed all sense of who she was in God. He had to drag her up to her feet and make her stand on His promises—His grace and mercies that were hers all along. Which she knew, but sometimes God allowed things to happen as a reminder.

Sherry remembered when she thought her father might die. He hadn't looked after himself, and the doctors had diagnosed bowel cancer. He'd been suffering for a while and never said a word. She could honestly say that was a low point in her life, losing Adrian, and then potentially losing her father. She didn't think she had the strength to withstand the heartache.

* * *

"Sherry, I want you to go to my safe."

"Dad, why don't you get some rest? You're tired." Sherry was sitting beside his bed, as was the routine every evening before he drifted off to sleep. She held his hand and took in his face. Where it used to be full and vibrant with a smooth chocolate complexion, it was now drawn and tired. His hair was peppered with grey, his face strained and there were dark circles under his eyes due to lack of sleep, but he was still a handsome man.

He'd lost so much weight due to the chemotherapy. He'd been overcome with vomiting. Some days he just couldn't eat, and she was worried. It saddened her to see him this way. He'd lost the light in his eyes and had given up.

"Please, Sherry. There's some paperwork in there. Bring them to me."

She sighed and reluctantly crossed the room to the painting of a ship moored on a vast body of water. She'd never liked the painting; it seemed dead, as if life had paused. Not even the sea had any movement. It was like her life; she supposed. Still and inert. She went home every night to an empty house. She didn't even have a pet to greet her because she travelled so much. Her life had paused.

She pulled the painting away, and behind was the safe embedded in the wall. After punching in the combination, she pulled out the papers and handed them to him, knowing what the next conversation would be.

"This is my will. Everything is in your name—"

"Dad, why are we having this conversation? You need to fight this thing. I won't entertain conversations about death. I won't have it." She felt tears sting her eyes. She loved her father. She only had wonderful memories of love and laughter growing up. He always had time for her as a child, and she remembered special moments when he would pull her onto his lap and hold her while he worked. She loved when they had family time out and visited their local park.

She remembered the pain and hurt she'd felt when he left, deciding to move to America after the divorce. She resented her mother for a while after he'd gone, and used to beg her to take him back. Sherry never really understood what had happened between them. Neither wanted to talk about it.

He took a deep breath. His breathing was laboured and shallow. "We must talk about it. It is going to happen."

"But not now." She sighed. "Okay, I promise to talk about it, if you promise to talk about what happens in your afterlife."

He was silent for a moment seeming to contemplate what she'd suggested. When she was a child, they went to church as a family, but stopped during her teenage years. He'd refused to step back inside a church, and she wondered if he resented God. He usually avoided talking about it, and already she could see a stubborn look enter his eyes and a swift downturn to his mouth.

"Okay, what did you want to talk about?" he asked.

"Well, according to you, you're going to…die." She found it difficult just saying the word.

He nodded.

"Do you know where you're going?"

"No, how would I know that?" He looked away. "Don't bother me with such things."

"Why? If it's inevitable, as you're saying, then there's one of two places your spirit will end up, and I want you to be with our Lord in heaven. Please listen to me."

He looked at her again. "I'm listening, Sherry, but I don't know what you want me to say. What will be, will be. I need to sort out my affairs here. I need to ensure you and Angela are taken care of." He coughed then heaved in a laboured breath. "It's important. I don't want to waste time talking about such things."

"But don't you see? Where you spend eternity is so much more important than anything on this earth."

He took in another deep breath. "That may be, but we need to discuss my will."

She ignored him and caught his hand. "What happened, Daddy? Why did you stop going to church?"

Her father looked at her for a long moment, then tears came to his eyes and he looked away.

"What is it? What's wrong?"

He was silent for a moment, seeming reluctant to say, then heaved a deep sigh and said; "He took my brother."

"Uncle Stephen?"

"Yes. Stephen was married for only two weeks. Brandy was pregnant with his baby girl, and He took him, just like that, like his life wasn't worth anything. How can I love a God who would do that?" Tears rolled down his cheeks.

She remembered when her Uncle Stephen died. He and Dad were close, and when Stephen passed, Dad was never the same. She realised this must have been the reason he'd moved to Atlanta, to help support his niece. And all the while, he'd resented God.

Shocked for a moment, she digested what he'd revealed and was suddenly afraid for him. How could he be angry at God? She only knew a loving and merciful Heavenly Father. How could anyone be angry at Him? "I didn't know. That's a long time to be angry, Dad."

"Stephen had a life. He had just gotten married. He had a baby on the way. How was that fair?"

"I don't know the mysteries of God, but maybe Uncle Stephen had fulfilled his purpose here on earth. Maybe he'd fulfilled everything he was supposed to do."

"And what was that? Leaving his wife a widow, alone and unsupported?"

"But Aunt Brandy was supported. You supported her and Chelsea, and now, Aunt Brandy is married again and happy."

"He was twenty-four, Sherry, your age. He hadn't lived *yet. It was wrong."*

"It is the enemy that steals, kills, and destroys. God wouldn't have caused that car accident. It wasn't God that took Stephen's life that day."

"So why didn't He protect Stephen? Why did He allow him to die?"

She could see the pain in her father's eyes. He seemed tortured. "Uncle Stephen wasn't a believer, Dad."

"So is God so harsh that he would remove his hand of protection just because someone made a mistake, just because they did not bow down to him?"

Sherry took a moment to pray. She needed to get through to him. She didn't want her dad to die and not have a place in heaven.

Lord, help me to explain. Help me to say the right words to convince him. Soften his heart.

"You're my father and I love you. You've always been there for me. You promised to always be there, always protect me, provide for me, give me everything I needed. But what if I rejected you and told you I did not want anything to do you with you? What if I turned my back on you and said I wanted to do my own thing? How would you feel?"

"I would be hurt, but I wouldn't stop being your father."

"Yes, exactly. God allows us to have free will. We choose the path we follow, and it says in the Bible that every person that lives on this earth will be given an opportunity to turn to Him before they die. Stephen would have been given that opportunity, and it was up to him to choose whether to take it or not."

"But does that mean he deserved to die?"

"No, it means that God can't protect someone who doesn't believe in Him. We don't know what happened before Uncle Stephen passed, he may have chosen to commit his spirit to God, he may have taken that opportunity." She squeezed his hand. "God loves you, Dad. He's giving you the opportunity now. Make things right with Him. Understand

that God is merciful and would not have taken Stephen's life. He is a wonderful and loving God."

Dad said nothing for a moment, looking sad and disheartened.

"You know God's word." She reached into her handbag, desperately needing to get through to him. She pulled out her Bible, and turned to John 14:6. "I am the way and the truth and the life. No one comes to the Father except through me.' You know that, don't you, Dad?"

"Yes, I am aware."

"You need to give your heart to Him, make things right with Him before you die. Please, Dad."

"Does it really matter?"

"Yes, it does." Tears came to her eyes and rolled down her cheeks. She had to convince him. "It matters to me, Dad, please. I'm begging you." She leaned forward and buried her face into his chest. "Please, Daddy…"

He raised a shaky hand and gently patted her head. She looked up at him, feeling guilty that she'd become so emotional, but she'd been holding it in for such a long time.

He took in a deep breath that seemed to take all his energy to muster, then closed his eyes for a moment. When he opened them again, they were filled with sadness and misted with tears. "I don't know how."

Her heart tripped. Will he finally submit to Him? "I'll show you. Will you pray with me?" She brushed the tears from her eyes, but more came.

He nodded.

"Say this prayer with me: Dear Lord Jesus, I know that I am a sinner, and I ask for Your forgiveness. I believe You died for my sins and rose from the dead." He repeated her

words with tears pouring down his cheeks, and she couldn't stop her own. "I turn from my sins and believe they are forgiven, and invite You to come into my heart and life..." She paused to brush at her tears, so overwhelmed with emotion. "And I want to trust and follow You as my Lord and Saviour."

After he repeated the prayer, he sobbed, and all she could do was hold him, so, so thankful that God had answered her prayer. She knew now for sure that her father would have a place in heaven.

<u>17</u>

Sherry sighed and glanced out at the view over the valley, reminded of the pain of that time with her father, but also the joy. "Thankfully, he pulled through. He's in remission."

"And you supported him on your own?"

She looked at Adrian, wondering at his line of thought. "Yes, I was all he had at the time. Angela was too young. And having to run his company wasn't easy."

Her father was pleased with her work and wanted her to move to Atlanta. She'd been thinking about it for years and was undecided, although she'd applied for a green card. It made things easier, especially with her travelling back and forth so often. But now that she was finally able to have some closure with Adrian, in retrospect, the prospect of relocating to Atlanta had become so much more appealing.

"I was worried about you coping on your own with all that. I wanted to support you. I was prepared to drop everything for you and join you in Atlanta, but you left. I need to understand why, Sherry."

She could see the pain and hurt in his eyes and felt the guilt return. She'd never considered how much her leaving might have hurt him. She'd thought he planned to marry Genevieve all along. They'd argued over it, after all. Her insecurities had fuelled her decision. She hadn't been sure she could trust him. "How's your mother?"

He frowned. "My mother is fine. She's a great help with the girls. You haven't answered my question, Sherry."

"Your mother told me to go."

"What?"

"She didn't feel I was good enough for you. She told me you planned to marry Genevieve, and then you did."

"*Because you left me*," he said incredulously.

"You told me there wasn't anything between you, yet, not too long after I left, you were walking down the aisle!" She felt the anger and hurt rise within her. She thought she'd dealt with her emotions, but clearly she hadn't.

"You knew I had a relationship with Genevieve before I met you."

"Yes, I did, but it was only thanks to your mother that I found out about your engagements, as you did not tell me. I think your mother knows more about who you are than you do, Adrian, and it scared me. She would never have accepted me, and she felt I would ruin your life. I didn't want to leave. But I didn't want to ruin your life, and she said Genevieve was waiting for you to make the right choice, and I was stopping that from happening. So I figured I would leave. And if you loved me, you would come for me. But you never did, and you married Genevieve, just as your mother said."

He stared at her for a long time, a deeply pained look came to his eyes and then he looked away.

She took in a breath. It felt like a burden had finally been released. She'd told him what she'd held inside for so long.

"So you're trying to say that my mother *made* you do it?"

"According to your mother, you already had plans to marry, Adrian. I wasn't going to stand in your way, and it turned out she was right."

"If this is true, why didn't you tell me?"

"What was the point? So you could try to hide the truth, as you are now? You should have been honest with me from the beginning." She sighed. "You made a choice to be with Genevieve. If you loved me, you wouldn't have married her."

"You didn't give me a chance. I planned to follow you. I just needed some time. It was a huge step. I had a lot hanging in the balance and my mother was pressuring me. I needed you to wait a little longer."

"How could I wait? My father was dying, Adrian!"

"I told you I would pay for his care—"

"And I couldn't not go. He needed me."

"*I needed you.*"

"And your mother wanted what she had planned, and I knew you wouldn't choose me over her."

His eyes narrowed. "So you're trying to say this is about my *mother*? This is a deflection. I don't believe you! What are you trying to hide from me?"

"You don't believe me?" She took in a breath. What else did she expect? Even after all the signs from his mother and the schemes and deceit, he still couldn't see it. "I guess I shouldn't be surprised." She reached into her rucksack and pulled out the neatly folded cheque that she'd kept all these years in preparation for this conversation. She'd brought it with her on every trip she made to Jamaica just in case she happened to meet him there. She handed it to him. "She tried to pay me off. I never cashed the cheque. You can give it back to her. I was never after your money, which is what she accused me of."

Adrian looked at the cheque for a long time, and she felt sorry for him, because he would finally have to see his mother for who she really was.

When he looked at her again, his eyes were tormented. "I-I didn't know," he said quietly.

"Well…sometimes it's good to know the truth."

"It's time to head back now," the tour guide called out.

Sherry stood to pack away her things, but Adrian caught her arm. "We need to talk."

"Do we?"

"Yes." His eyes beseeched hers.

He was still holding her arm, and she felt the electrical current skim along her skin. She was reminded of how wonderful he was, how intense their love was, and the need that had always been between them.

"Okay, let's talk."

* * *

"You're beautiful. You know that."

She smiled, looking at him directly. "Why? Because I gave your dinner to that homeless guy? I thought you might have been upset." She slipped her arms around his neck.

They'd taken a leisurely walk to their local restaurant, deciding to eat in but not wanting to cook. Besides, it was a warm night, and they wanted to get some fresh air. But on the way back, they'd seen a homeless man on the street with his dog. He hadn't begged or asked for money, but he was seated on the ground sharing his evening meal with his dog, which consisted of half a slice of bread, which he retrieved from his pocket. It was heart-breaking, and Sherry couldn't walk by and not provide any help.

She gave him their meal and began to reach into her purse, but Adrian stopped her, emptying his wallet and giving the money to the man. Her heart swelled with love.

"No, why would I? He needed it more than I did. What you did was a good thing. That's why I love you. Your heart is beautiful."

Sherry smiled, and then she kissed him, thanking God for being so gracious in bringing someone so loving and special into her life.

* * *

They argued.

In the past, they'd never argued, so this was new. Only that one time after Miriam's revelation, and funnily enough, their argument continued on from that moment, as it had been the catalyst that ended their relationship. The trust they'd shared had been broken, and their love for each other was clearly not strong enough to withstand it.

The rest of the group went ahead of them, and they hung back and bickered the whole way down the mountain. Adrian was angry and resentful that she'd left him, and she was angry and resentful at his mother, and him for not coming for her.

"You left! What did you expect me to do?"

"You could have at least waited, Adrian. If you loved me as you said you did, then you wouldn't have just married someone else—while still engaged to me, I might add!"

"You left knowing the pressure I was under. I had to make a choice."

"Ahh, yes, the choice that never included me from the very beginning! Let's not pretend."

"You left me! I asked you not to go, and you totally disregarded my feelings! As far as I was concerned, you didn't want me. You had already decided before you left that it was over, don't *pretend* with me. You want to talk about honesty? Who isn't being honest now? You said you would call me. You never did. What did you expect me to do?"

"Get on a plane and support your fiancée! You knew what I was going through, weeks of chemotherapy, terrified my father might die, trying to run a company with minimal experience and the obstacles I had to battle. It was a difficult time—" She stopped, realising this was not getting anywhere, it was pointless. She'd seen the evidence of anger and what happened in the spiritual realm, and this needed to end right now.

Sherry whispered a prayer of forgiveness. This was never her intention, and she thought she'd forgiven him a long time ago. Clearly she hadn't, and she understood now why they'd needed to meet again. "Adrian, please, can we call a truce? I'm sorry for leaving in the way I did. I'm sorry for everything. I shouldn't have listened to your mother, but I was afraid she was telling the truth. And when you got married, as far as I was concerned, it *was* the truth. I'm sorry, okay? I can't do this with you. I want closure and to move on. I have never moved on, Adrian."

"So you want to rid me from your life, as you did before?"

"Have you not heard anything I said?"

"Yes, I heard you. You believed my mother's lies, instead of coming to me and loving me the way you said you did, and believing in *me* and *my* love."

She stared at him, tears coming to her eyes. "I'm sorry. I'm sorry for hurting you and not believing in you." She slipped to the ground, exhausted and drained from all the arguing, for loving this man for fifteen years but not being able to even hear his voice, and now, seeing him after all these years, to discover that he hated her. It was too much to bear. The dam burst, and she began to sob with deep, soul-wrenching cries.

After a moment, he knelt beside her. "Sherry, I'm sorry…" He sat down and pulled her into his arms.

The tour guide came rushing over. "Is everything okay? Is she hurt?"

"She's fine. She just needs a moment. You go ahead. We know the trail."

"I know you do, but I would lose my job if I left you up here alone." The tour guide sighed. "I'll ask the others to take a break, but don't be long—we have to meet the bus on time." She walked away, leaving them alone again.

Sherry tucked her face into his neck and inhaled. Oh, how she'd missed him, missed his scent, his strong arms—missed being held tightly like this. *My Lord Jesus, my way maker, please…oh, please.*

"Sherry. I didn't mean to upset you. Please stop crying. You're making me feel guilty. I'm not ready to let go of the hurt I've felt all these years…"

And then she heard the words that she'd been waiting for.

"I'm sorry. I should have come for you. And I'm sorry for my mother."

She eased back so she could look at him. He had tears in his eyes, and it made her want to cry some more. She sighed. "Well, there is one good thing that has come out of this, and that is…you have a lovely family." She wiped her tears. "I always prayed you would be happy."

He looked at her but didn't say anything for a moment. "For a while I hurt badly after you left. I couldn't face a life without you. But then my feelings for Genevieve grew into love. And yes, we have two lovely girls."

It hurt to hear him say he loved someone else. She always thought she would be his only love. "Well…I've been hurting for fifteen years. I never got over you, Adrian. My only hope now is for us to have some closure, so I can finally move on with my life." She reluctantly pulled away, not wanting to leave the safe haven of his arms, and stood, conscious of the tour guide becoming impatient.

Adrian stood too. "That's all you want? Closure?"

She looked away, ignoring his question, because it wasn't the truth. She rummaged in her rucksack for a tissue. "She's pretty. They have her looks, but they have your smile." She dabbed at her face.

He gave a wry smile, and there was pain in his eyes. "Yes, they have my smile and their mother's looks. But who's pretty?"

"Your wife."

He gave her a strange look. "Genevieve died, Sherry. A year ago now."

Her heart tripped. *He's a widower?* "Oh, I didn't know. I'm sorry."

"To ensure there are no further misunderstandings between us, the lady I am with is the girl's aunt, my sister-in-law. So, I ask again, is closure all you want?"

Sherry's heart leapt at the look in his eyes—the need and love for her that had never left, and then she did what she'd wanted to do all along: she flung her arms around his neck and kissed him.

The End

If you enjoyed *Forever in my Heart*, I would be so grateful if you could spare five minutes and leave a review, your support really means a lot.

Author Note

Dear Reader,

I felt compelled to write this story, of Sherry and Adrian's love for each other. But I also wanted to show Sherry's relationship with our Lord, and how He intervenes in our lives. Although my name appears on the cover of this book, this one came from Him. There are so many aspects of the Christian walk, and there are so many that are forgotten.

Sometimes we go about our lives and are unaware of what happens behind the scenes. God is always there; nudging us, protecting us, setting us on a path He directs—always a constant. What a mighty and amazing God we serve! He is the air that I breathe. And there is always so much more in Him.

God is extending the fullness of who He is to you today. A life filled with blessings in abundance. You only need to take it.

In Romans 10:9-10 it says that, "If you declare with your mouth, 'Jesus is Lord,' and believe in your heart that God raised him from the dead, you will be saved. For it is with your heart that you believe and are justified, and it is with your mouth that you profess your faith and are saved."

I urge you to take this step today, to get to know Him personally. Understand who He is as a person and all the wonders He has for you.

The power of God is a gift; we don't do anything to deserve it or do good works to obtain it. It is also a manifestation of His love for us. It is my prayer for you to receive all the gifts He wishes to bestow upon you.

Thank you for your support and taking the time to read *Forever in my Heart*. I sincerely hope it blessed you as much as it blessed me to write it.

Dionne Grace

Coming Soon...

Circumstances push Samyra and Joshua together, forcing them both to re-evaluate their plans, their goals, their everything…

Discover how their love develops in Book 5 of The Vision of Love series, **HEAVEN'S GIFT.**

Shauna hates storms. Brandon rescues her one dark night and she sweeps him off his feet, turning his life upside down. He isn't prepared for Shauna— and he isn't prepared for the storm she creates within him…

Discover how Brandon rides the storm in Book 1 of The Unmerited Grace series, **A STORMY CONCEPTION**

Christine never stopped loving Andrew, but he is her past and she isn't prepared to open old wounds. She has moved on and she wants things to remain that way.

Will Andrew remain in her past? Find out in Book 2 of The Unmerited Grace series, **A LOVE LOST**

"I am yours, and you are mine..." It has always been that way between them, from the very first moment of love.

Kyle thinks his dreams have come true when he marries Faye. But soon they discover that their wants—never mind their needs—are the least of the challenges that lie ahead for them. Will her love remain his for always? Find out in Book 3 of the Howard Family series, **MINE FOR ALWAYS.**

**Join my mailing list for updates and the release dates.
www.dionnegrace.com**

Book 1

The Vision of Love Series

Excerpt from When Two Love As One

Rachel is not interested in another relationship and David wants a wife. She is the answer to his prayers, and being an impatient man, used to getting what he wants, he won't let her go.

She returned her gaze to his. "What did the Holy Spirit tell you about me…about us?"

David averted his eyes, taken aback by her question. What could he say without revealing what the Holy Spirit had told him?

"You want more than just friendship, don't you?" she asked, pressing him.

He returned his gaze to hers. He wanted a whole lot more than he'd realised—the attraction between them was too strong. "Yes."

Rachel guessed as much. She could feel it. "David…I can't be anything more than your friend." Her voice was gentle; she didn't want to hurt his feelings. "I'm sorry." She felt a nudge inside her from the Holy Spirit. She ignored it.

"Why can't we be more than that? We are very much attracted to each other, there is no denying that, and you are a very beautiful woman, Rachel."

His eyes darkened and became intense, making it difficult to keep eye contact. Her heart began to pound under the heat of his gaze, and she looked away for a moment, glancing around the busy restaurant at the other couples enjoying romantic interludes, and she wanted to keep well away from anything near romance. Yes, the attraction was strong, but it wasn't something she would entertain or consider. "Because I'm not looking for a relationship right now."

"When will you be?"

She laughed. "Never!"

He raised a brow, but did not join in with her laughter.

Her smile faded and she sighed. He was clearly irked by her response, hence the reason why she did not encourage friendships with men. It always resulted in her letting them down, their egos so bruised that she never saw them again. It was a shame, because she really liked David and knew she could learn a lot from him. "I'm sorry. I don't mean to make light of your interest in me. You're a very attractive man. I'm sure there are many women out there who would want your attention."

"Ahh, but they're not you, Rachel."

"Oh, I'm nothing special, believe me. I already have a failed marriage under my belt and have no intention of ever going down that road again." She paused for a moment. "And you strike me as a man who does not have casual relationships."

"And you do?"

She chuckled. "I don't have those either!" She looked over at him guiltily, as he clearly did not see the humorous side of this and wanted her to take him seriously. "Look, David, I don't want there to be any misconceptions between us, so I'll be as honest with you as I can." She paused, lifting her glass to sip her water. "I had a very unhappy marriage—nineteen long years. I did the right thing as a Christian woman and remained in a loveless marriage, feeling trapped and suffocated. When we got divorced, I was so relieved, happy for the first time in years. I'm free and at peace, and I want to stay this way." She held his gaze, ensuring he clearly understood her. "I'm damaged goods. I'm very much scarred. I could never trust you."

When Two Love As One
Available Now

Excerpt from For Eternity

When you discover your purpose is to save someone's life, what do you do?

That is the question Lanya Bowden asks herself when she meets Ryan Chapman. She has a purpose to fulfil—there is no escaping it, but Ryan has been hurt. He fights the attraction then finally has to give in. As always, nothing is ever straightforward, and there are a few ups and downs between them.

After the short walk to the club, and back in the warmth, he pulled her aside in an alcove in the darkened corridor. "I want to see you again."

She slipped off his jacket and handed it to him. "You have my number."

She went to walk away, but he stopped her, placing a hand on her arm. "I'm attracted to you, and you're obviously attracted to me—"

"What makes you think I'm attracted to you?"

He could see the teasing amusement in her eyes. "You gave me your number." He shrugged on his jacket.

"Because you wanted it."

He smiled. She was feisty. He liked that. "If I touch you right now, I know you'll melt in my arms."

Her eyes grew serious. "Don't play with me."

He wanted to kiss her.

He searched her eyes, reading what had been evident from the very beginning. He reached out, sliding his fingers into her hair, caressing her cheek. His touch was gentle, and she was receptive; her eyes darkened, and she stepped a little closer to him, resting her hands against his chest. He leaned in to kiss her, but at that moment, a couple burst in through the side entrance, howling in laughter, clearly inebriated. A gust of cool wind entered in their wake, and the moment was lost as they broke away.

"Who is that guy you were with?"

Lanya sighed. "He's my ex, and he won't accept that it's over between us. I ended things with him a year ago. He turned up here just to be difficult. You don't need to worry about him." She eased back. "I've got to get back to my friends. Call me," she said, walking away.

He had a distinct feeling of abandonment and fought the urge to follow.

He made his way back to his group, his mind filled with Lanya, surprised at his impulse, but disappointed that he wasn't able to follow through.

She left after a while. He watched as she said her goodbyes, her ex sticking close by her side. She looked over at Ryan just before she disappeared and waved at him, then turned and made her way through the throng of gyrating bodies.

His mind filtered to the conversation his friends were having, but he wasn't really engaged, and when the topic switched to making plans to stop at a strip club, that was his cue to leave.

He headed out and pushed his way back through the crowd, exiting at the side door. He flicked up his collar and buttoned up his jacket against the cool night air.

"Got a light, mate?" a man asked as Ryan rounded the corner of the street.

Leaned up in the alcove to a boarded-up building, the man stood with someone who appeared to be his partner in crime. They both looked rough. Their clothes were dirty and there was a faint smell of stale alcohol that seemed to hover in the air around them. Ryan shook his head and noted in his peripheral vision when the man motioned to the other to follow.

Great. He could do without hassle tonight.

The road was deserted but for a handful of pedestrians on the other side of the street and a few cars zipping by. He looked at his watch. Eleven forty-five. He hadn't meant to stay out this long, and being in Central London, parking was scarce, so he'd taken the underground, and now it was way too late for public transport. Waiting for a night bus would take an age, and he wanted to get home. His only option was a taxi.

He continued on, aware now that the men were following, the sounds of their footsteps coming nearer.

He turned and stepped back as one blocked his path and the other stood behind, then Ryan noticed the knife in the man's hand.

His heart pounded with fear, adrenaline rushing through his veins.

"Hand over your money," the man demanded. His eyes were cold, shifting around, taking note of the other pedestrians on the street. He concealed the weapon in his hand, but at the ready to knife Ryan with it.

Ryan's heart was pounding so hard now he could hear it. He could feel the presence of the other man, ready to pounce if he didn't do what they asked. He looked around; there wasn't anyone near enough who could help even if he shouted. And if he took out his wallet, would it end there, or would they stab him anyway? The latter was more likely, and his breathing became erratic. His mother's words filtered through his brain.

Life is short…

Was this it for him? Life over?

But he hadn't achieved anything big, no acclaimed glory—no wealth. What did he have to show for his life? He wasn't ready to die.

Lord, please help me.

"Hand it over, now!" the man shouted, agitated. He shifted, his arm moving swiftly, about to strike.

Ryan felt as if time slowed and he was observing, watching his life come to an end. His final moments on this earth, and what had he done?

Nothing of significance.

The headlines would say, *A thirty-nine-year-old man, divorcé and father of one, found dead in a pool of blood…*

Then Ryan felt a presence. He wasn't sure what it was. He saw the flash of the blade in the man's hand as it shot forward, aiming for his abdomen, but instead of connecting with his body as expected, it hit a wall in front of him, as if there was someone standing there, an invisible presence.

It happened so fast, and the man behind went to grab him and was thrown to the ground.

There was a clang as the knife fell and a look of shock and terror crossed the man's face, then he ran off down the street. The other man followed soon after.

Ryan couldn't see it, but he felt it. God's presence. There was an angel protecting him. He didn't know how he knew this, but the angel was there.

That was when he knew that it wasn't his time, and with definitive clarity, he finally understood that life was short…

For Eternity
Available Now

Also by Dionne Grace

The Vision of Love Series.

MY HEART WHISPERS
WHEN TWO LOVE AS ONE
WHEN TWO BECOME ONE
COMMITTED TO LOVE
RESOLUTE LOVE

Howard Family Series

GIFTED LOVE
IF ONLY...

The Faith Series

FAITHFULLY AGAIN
FAITHFUL SURRENDER

God's Perfect Timing Series

TIME TO NEED

Individual Titles

MAYBE NOW
MAYBE FOREVER
A CHRISTMAS PRAYER
MISSING YOU FOR CHRISTMAS
FOR ETERNITY

About the Author

Dionne Grace is a romantic at heart. She loves reading books, which in her early teenage years enhanced her vivid imagination. She would often invent fascinating love stories to entertain her school friends involving famous pop stars. She used to scribble notes on the back of school books while her teacher's backs were turned! Her friends loved it, and remind her of it to this day!

She loves to write and when she is not writing, she is reading and juggles this with her full-time job.

She writes sweet romances, about couples in relationships who have a passion for each other. Sometimes this passion leads them into situations where they lose themselves, taking them down a path which possibly they should not have gone down, or in contrast, through life's experiences; they reject the love that is offered, not having the faith or forgiveness to trust it.

Her books are intentionally thought provoking, and real life. A message about a discovery of how the scars of life can be healed, no matter how difficult this sometimes seems in this imperfect world. And ultimately, through God's divine intervention he imparts a revelation of what his purpose was all along.

As you must have guessed, she has a love for God and everything spiritual; she hopes this shines through in her books.

www.dionnegrace.com

www.ingramcontent.com/pod-product-compliance
Lightning Source LLC
Chambersburg PA
CBHW061254120726
48001CB00001B/295